Meg Cabot is the author of the phenomenally successful The Princess Diaries series. With vast numbers of copies sold around the world, the books have topped the US and UK bestseller lists for weeks and won several awards. Two movies based on the series have been massively popular throughout the world.

Meg is also the author of the bestselling *All American Girl*, *All American Girl: Ready or Not*, *How to Be Popular*, *Jinx*, *Teen Idol*, *Avalon High*, The Mediator series and the Allie Finkle series as well as many other books for teenagers and adults. She and her husband divide their time between Florida and Indiana.

Visit Meg Cabot's website at
www.megcabot.co.uk

Books by Meg Cabot

The Princess Diaries series

The Mediator series

All American Girl
All American Girl: Ready or Not

Avalon High
Avalon High manga: The Merlin Prophecy
Teen Idol
How to Be Popular
Jinx
Tommy Sullivan Is a Freak
Nicola and the Viscount
Victoria and the Rogue
Airhead

For younger readers

Allie Finkle's Rules for Girls: Moving Day
Allie Finkle's Rules for Girls: The New Girl

For older readers

The Guy Next Door
Boy Meets Girl
Every Boy's Got One
Queen of Babble
Size 12 Is Not Fat
Size 14 Is Not Fat Either

Also available in audio

The Princess Diaries

To The Nines

Meg Cabot

MACMILLAN

First published 2007 by Macmillan Children's Books

This edition published 2008 by Macmillan Children's Books
a division of Macmillan Publishers Limited
20 New Wharf Road, London N1 9RR
Basingstoke and Oxford
Associated companies throughout the world
www.panmacmillan.com

ISBN 978-0-330-44855-0

Copyright © Meg Cabot LLC 2007

The right of Meg Cabot to be identified as the
author of this work has been asserted by her in accordance
with the Copyright, Designs and Patents Act 1988.

1 3 5 7 9 8 6 4 2

A CIP catalogue record for this book is available from
the British Library.

Typeset by Intype Libra Ltd
Printed and bound in the UK by CPI Mackays, Chatham ME5 8TD

For Sarah Davies, an extraordinary editor,
with love and thanks

Many thanks to Beth Ader, Jennifer Brown, Barbara Cabot, Sarah Davies, Michele Jaffe, Laura Langlie, Amanda Maciel, Abigail McAden and especially Benjamin Egnatz.

'Ah, yes, Your Royal Highness,' she said. 'We are princesses I believe. At least, one of us is.'

Sara felt the blood rush up into her face. She only just saved herself. If you were a princess, you did not fly into rages.

'It's true,' she said. 'Sometimes I do pretend I am a princess. I pretend I am a princess so I can try to behave like one.'

A Little Princess
Frances Hodgson Burnett

Friday, September 10, 9 p.m., *Beauty and the Beast*, Lunt-Fontanne Theater Ladies' Lounge

He hasn't called. I just checked with Mom.

I don't think it's completely fair of her to accuse me of believing the entire world revolves around my break-up with Michael. Because I don't. Really. How was I supposed to know she'd just gotten Rocky down for the night? She should turn off the ringer if he's turning into that much of a problem sleeper.

Anyway, there were no messages.

I guess I shouldn't have expected there to be. I mean, I checked on his flight, and he's not due to arrive in Japan for another seventeen hours.

And you aren't allowed to use cellphones or PDAs while you're actually in the air. At least, not for calls or text-messaging.

Or answering emails.

But that's OK. Really, it is. He'll call.

He'll get my email and then he'll call and we'll make up and everything will go back to normal.

It *has* to.

In the meantime, I just have to go on as if things *are* normal. Well, as normal as things can be while waiting to hear back from your boyfriend of two years with whom you've broken up, but to whom you sent an apology email because you realized you were completely and unequivocally wrong.

Especially since if you don't get back together you know you'll only live a sort of half life and be destined to have a series of meaningless relationships with supermodels.

1

Oh, wait. That's my dad. Never mind.

But, you know. It's me too. Minus the supermodels.

Watching *Beauty and the Beast* tonight with J.P. has made me realize how completely stupid I've been this past week.

Not that I hadn't realized it already. But the show *really* drove it home.

Which is especially weird, since Michael and I have never exactly seen eye to eye on the theatre. I mean, I could barely get Michael ever even to *go* with me to see the kind of shows I like, which are primarily ones involving girls in hoop skirts and things that fly down from the ceiling of the theatre (such as *The Phantom of the Opera* and *Tarzan: The Musical*).

And on the few occasions he DID go with me, he spent the whole time leaning over and whispering, 'I can see why this show is closing. No guy would really stand around singing to a talking teapot about how much he likes some girl. You know that, don't you? And where is the full orchestra supposed to be coming from? I mean, they're in a dungeon. It just doesn't make any sense.'

Which I used to think actually ruined the whole experience. As did Michael's excusing himself every five minutes to go to the men's room on the pretence of having drunk too much water at dinner. But really he was just checking for *World of Warcraft* alerts on his cellphone.

But even though I'm having a nice time here with J.P. and all, I can't help wishing Michael was here to complain that *Beauty and the Beast* is just a cheesy Disney musical targeted at little kids, who are hardly discriminating viewers, and that the music's really bad and the whole thing is just to get the tourists to spend money on expensive T-shirts, sippy cups and glossy theatre programmes.

It's especially sad he's not here, because I realized tonight that the story of *Beauty and the Beast* is really the story of Michael and me.

Not the beauty part (of course). And not the beast part either.

But the part about two people who start out being friends and don't even realize they like each other until it's almost too late . . .

That is totally us.

Except, of course, that Belle is smarter than I am. Like, would it really have mattered to Belle if the Beast, back before he ever held her captive in his castle, had hooked up with Judith Gershner, then failed to mention it?

No. Because that all happened BEFORE Belle and the Beast found each other. So what difference did it make?

Exactly: None.

I just can't believe how stupid I've been about all this. I swear, even cheesy as it is – and, OK, I have to admit, I can see the cheese factor in it now – *Beauty and the Beast* has brought new clarity to my life.

Which shouldn't be all that surprising since it is, after all, a tale as old as time.

Anyway, I know in the past I've said my ideal man is one who can sit through an entire performance of *Beauty and the Beast*, the most romantic and beautiful story ever told, and not snicker in the wrong places (such as when the Beast is undergoing his onstage transformation into the Prince, or when the fake stuffed wolves come out – well, they can't make them TOO scary, since there are little kids in the audience).

But now I realize that the only guy I've ever attended the show with who has passed that test is J.P. Reynolds-Abernathy the Fourth. He even – I couldn't help noticing – had a single tear trickling down his cheek during the scene where Beauty valiantly exchanges her own life for her father's.

Michael has never cried during a Broadway show. Except in that scene where Tarzan's ape father is brutally murdered.

And that was only because he was laughing so hard.

But here's the thing: and I'm starting to think that isn't necessarily a bad thing. I think guys just might be *different* from girls. Not just because they actually care about stuff like whether or not there'll ever be a *The Nightstalkers* movie starring Jessica Biel, reprising her role as Abby Whistler from *Blade: Trinity*.

Or because they think it's OK to sleep with Judith Gershner and never mention it to their girlfriend because it happened before they started going out.

But because they are just *programmed* differently. Like to be unmoved by the sight of a guy in a gorilla suit getting pretend-shot onstage.

Whereas they completely fall for that scene in the movie *Notting Hill* where Julia Roberts's character goes back to that guy played by Hugh Grant, even though in a million years a snotty movie star like that would never fall for a lowly bookstore owner.

And I say that as a princess who is in love with a college student.

The thing is, I finally get it now: guys are different than we are.

But that's not always a bad thing. In fact, as my ancestors would say, *Vive la différence*. Because, OK, a lot of guys don't like musicals.

But those same guys might also give you a snowflake necklace for your fifteenth birthday to represent the non-denominational winter dance where you first declared your love for one another.

Which, you have to admit, is way romantic.

Oh. The lights just flickered. It's time to go back to my seat for the second act.

Which, truthfully, I'm not really looking forward to. It would be OK if J.P. didn't keep asking me if I'm all right.

I totally get that he's concerned about me as a friend and all, but – what does he expect me to say? How can he not know that the answer is no, I'm *not* all right? Do I need to remind him that not two nights ago I idiotic-ally ripped OFF that snowflake necklace and THREW it at the guy who gave it to me? Does he think you just automatically rebound from something like that, just because you are attending a musical with dancing teacups in it?

J.P. is totally sweet, but he's a little clueless some-times.

Although Tina is completely right, it turns out: J.P. really *is* a pent-up volcano of passion. The single tear proves it. All he needs is the right woman to unlock his heart – which up until now he has kept in a cold, hard shell for his own emotional protection – and he will explode like the simmering caldera that makes up part of Yellowstone National Park.

And obviously this woman wasn't Lilly (who by the way also hasn't called or emailed me, even to yell at me some more for being a boyfriend-stealer. Which isn't a bit like her).

On the other hand, maybe J.P. isn't clueless. Maybe he's just a guy.

They can't all be like the Beast, I guess.

Friday, September 10, 11.45 p.m., the Loft

Inbox: 0
No phone messages either.

But Michael's plane is still in the air for another fourteen and a quarter hours. He'll call me when he lands.

I mean, he *has* to. Right?

OK, not thinking about that now. Because every time I do, I get these weird heart palpitations and my palms get sweaty.

Meanwhile, a hand-delivered envelope *did* arrive for me while I was gone. Mom told me about it (not very happily) when I woke her up to ask if Michael had called (honestly, I didn't realize she was asleep. Usually she's up watching *David Letterman* until the musical guest comes on at twelve thirty. How was I supposed to know the musical guest was Fergie, so Mom went to bed early?).

The hand-delivered envelope obviously wasn't from Michael. It was on fancy ivory stationery and had a big red wax seal with the letters D and R stamped in the middle. There was something about it that just screamed Grandmere.

So I wasn't very surprised when Mom said, all crabbily, 'Your grandmother says to open it right away.'

I *was* surprised, however, when she added, 'And she said to call her when you do. No matter what time it is.'

'I'm supposed to call Grandmere *after eleven o'clock at night?*' This didn't make any sense. Grandmere goes to bed right before the eleven o'clock news every night without fail, unless she's out partying with Henry Kissinger or somebody like that. She says if she doesn't get her full eight hours of beauty sleep, she can't do a thing with the bags under her eyes the next day, no matter how much haemorrhoid cream she puts on them.

'That's the message,' Mom grumped, and pulled the covers back over her head (though how she can sleep with Mr Gianini snoring away like that next to her is a mystery to me. It can only be true love).

I wasn't liking the look of that envelope, and I *definitely* wasn't liking the idea of having to call Grandmere at eleven thirty at night.

But I went to my room and ripped open the seal and pulled out the letter and started reading . . .

And nearly had a heart attack.

I was on the phone with Grandmere in about two seconds flat.

'Oh, Amelia,' she said, sounding completely awake. 'Good. Finally. Did you receive your letter?'

'From Lana Weinberger's MOM?' I practically screamed. I only remembered to keep my voice down because I live in a loft and my little brother was sleeping in the next room and I didn't want to risk the wrath of Mom if I woke him up. 'Asking me to give the keynote speech at her women's society's big charity event to raise money for African orphans? Yes. But . . . how did you know? Did you get one too?'

'Don't be ridiculous,' she scoffed. 'I have my ways of finding out these things. Now, Amelia, I must know. This is very important. Did she mention issuing you an invitation to join the Domina Reis when you come of age?' You could practically hear her salivating, she was so excited. *'Did she say anything about asking you to pledge when you turn eighteen?'*

'Yes,' I said. 'But, Grandmere, I've never even heard of these Domina Reis before. And I don't have time for this right now. I am going through a very stressful time at the moment, and I really have to concentrate on just staying centred—'

This was totally the wrong thing to say, however. Grandmere was practically breathing fire when she replied in her princessiest tone, 'For your information, the Domina Rei is one of the most influential women's societies in the world. How can you not be aware of this, Amelia? They are like the Opus Dei of women's organizations. Only not religiously affiliated.'

I had to admit, this got me kind of interested, in spite of myself. 'Really? Opus Dei? That secret society in *The Da Vinci Code*? The one where the members whip themselves? Lana's mom keeps a weird metal spike wrapped around her leg?'

'Of course not,' Grandmere said with a sniff. 'I meant figuratively.'

This was disappointing to hear. I have never met Lana's mom (and she clearly knows nothing about me, because in her letter she mentioned how much Lana has appreciated my friendship over the years, and how regrettable it is that my busy royal agenda has kept me from attending more of the parties she knows Lana has invited me to at their place. Um. Yeah), but the idea of any member of the Weinberger family with possible spikes digging into her fills me with great joy.

'And,' Grandmere went on, 'I know I've told you about the Domina Reis before, Amelia. The Contessa Trevanni is a member.'

'Bella's grandmother?' Grandmere hasn't mentioned her arch-enemy the Contessa much since the

9

Contessa's granddaughter, Bella, delighted the entire Trevanni family by running off last Christmas with my pseudo-cousin Prince René and getting, well, knocked up by him (Grandmere says it's more polite to say *enceinte*, which is the French term, but the truth is, he really did knock her up. I mean, hello, has *no one* in my family heard of condoms?).

After a stern talking-to by my dad (and, I suspect, an exchange of cash: René was just days from signing a television deal for a new reality show, *Prince Charming*, in which a number of young single girls were to compete for the chance to date a real-life prince . . . namely, René), René finally married Bella. Sadly for her grandmother, the wedding took place in a quiet private ceremony, since René took so long to finally pop the question that Bella was obviously showing, and they're still sensitive about that kind of thing in *Majesty* magazine.

Now Bella and René are living on the Upper East Side in a penthouse the Contessa bought them as a wedding present, attending Lamaze classes together and looking as if neither of them could be happier.

Grandmere is so jealous that Bella got René instead of me – even though I'm still in *high school*, hello – she could plotz. Basically, we never speak of it.

'Audrey Hepburn was a Domina Rei, as well,' Grandmere went on. 'As well as Princess Grace of Monaco. Hillary Rodham Clinton. Supreme Court Justice Sandra Day O'Connor. Jacqueline Kennedy Onassis. Even Oprah Winfrey.'

A hush fell over our conversation then, as it always does in polite society whenever Ms Winfrey's name is mentioned.

Then I said, 'Well, that's all very nice, Grandmere. However, like I said, this really isn't the best time for me. I—'

But Grandmere, as usual, wasn't even listening.

'I, of course, was asked to join years ago. However, due to a complete misunderstanding involving a certain gentleman who shall remain nameless, I was ruthlessly blackballed.'

'Oh,' I said. 'Well, that's too bad. I—'

'Fine. If you must know, it was Prince Rainier of Monaco. But the rumours were completely false! I never even looked at him twice! Was it my fault he was so fascinated by me that he used to follow me around like a puppy? I can't imagine how anyone could have thought it was anything other than what it was . . . a simple infatuation a much older man bore for a young woman who couldn't help sparkling with wit and *joie de vivre*.'

It took me a minute to figure out who she was talking about. 'You mean . . . *you*?'

'Of course me, Amelia! What is wrong with you? Why do you think he married Grace Kelly? Why do you think his family allowed him to marry a movie actress? Only because they were so relieved he agreed to marry *anyone* after the heartbreak he experienced when I rejected him . . .'

I gasped. 'Grandmere! You turned him *gay*?'

'Of course not! Amelia, don't be ridiculous. I – Oh, never mind. How did we even get on this topic? The fact is, the Contessa Trevanni will eat her own head if you give the keynote address at her women's society's charity gala. They've never asked *her* granddaughter to speak. Of course, why would they? She's never

11

accomplished anything, except to get pregnant, which any halfwit can do, and she's such a namby-pamby, she'd probably freeze up at the sight of those two thousand impeccably groomed successful businesswomen staring up at her—'

I gasped again . . . but this time for a different reason. 'Wait . . . two *thousand*?'

'We'll have to make an appointment at Chanel right away,' Grandmere blathered on. 'Something subdued, I think, yet youthful. I do believe it's time we fitted you with a suit. Dresses are fine, but you can never go wrong with a really good wool suit—'

'Impeccably groomed, successful businesswomen?' I echoed, feeling slightly faint. 'I thought they were all like Lana's mom . . . society wives with full-time nannies and cooks and maids—'

'Nancy Weinberger is one of the most sought-after interior decorators in Manhattan,' Grandmere interrupted coldly. 'She completely furnished the apartment the Contessa bought for René and Bella. Let me see now, the Domina Reis colours are blue and white . . . blue's never been your best colour, but we'll have to make do . . .'

'Grandmere,' I said. Panic was rising in my throat. It was sort of the way I felt every time I thought about Michael, only without the sweaty palms. 'I can't do this. I can't give a speech in front of two thousand successful businesswomen. You don't understand – I'm going through a romantic crisis at the moment and, until it's resolved, I really think I need to keep a low profile . . . in fact, even after it's resolved I don't think I can speak in front of that many people.'

'Nonsense,' Grandmere said crisply. 'You spoke in

12

front of the Genovian Parliament about the parking meters, remember? As if any of us could forget.'

'Yeah, but they were just old guys in wigs, not Lana Weinberger's mom! I don't know about this, Grandmere. I think maybe I should—'

'Of course, Lord only knows what we'll do about your hair. I don't suppose it will have grown in by then. Maybe Paolo can fashion some sort of extensions. I'll phone him in the morning . . .'

'Seriously, Grandmere,' I said. 'I think I—'

But it was too late. She'd already hung up, still muttering about hair extensions.

Great. This is all I need.

Saturday, September 11, 9 a.m., the Loft

Inbox: 0

Which isn't weird. I mean, he's still got another five hours in the air. And then he has to go through customs.

So I just need to be patient. I just need to be calm. I just need to —

FtLouie: TINA!!!! ARE YOU THERE???? If you're there, write back. I AM DYING!!!!

>

Iluvromance: Hi, Mia! I'm here. Why are you dying?????

Oh, thank God. Thank God for Tina Hakim Baba.

FtLouie: Because while I know the bond Michael and I have is too strong to be torn asunder by a simple misunderstanding, and that he's going to call when he gets to Japan and tell me he forgives me and everything is going to be all right — what if it isn't? What if he doesn't? Oh, God — my palms won't stop sweating!!!!! And I think I might be having a heart attack . . .

>

Iluvromance: Mia! It's going to be all right! Of course Michael is going to forgive you! You guys will get back together, and everything is going to be just like it used to be. Better, even. Because couples who go through hard times together always come out stronger for it . . .

>

FtLouie: That's right! And whatever, right? My ancestresses have faced far harsher adversity. Such as marauding invaders and abductions and being forced to drink wine out of their murdered fathers' skulls and all that. Michael and I will be fine!

>

Iluvromance: Totally! So I take it you're not going tonight then?

>

FtLouie: Going to what?

>

Iluvromance: To the victory party.

>

FtLouie: What victory party?

>

Iluvromance: You know. Lilly and Perin's victory party. For winning the student election.

>

FtLouie: I wasn't invited to any victory party.

>

Iluvromance: You didn't get the email?
>
FtLouie: Noooooo . . .
>
Iluvromance: Oh.
>
FtLouie: Oh, what?
>
Iluvromance: I didn't think she was serious.
>
FtLouie: Who? What are you talking about?
>
Iluvromance: Lilly. She was saying she was
             never speaking to you again
             because you're a back-stabbing
             boyfriend stealer. But I thought
             she was joking.
>
!!!!!!
>
FtLouie: WHAT???? HOW CAN SHE SAY THAT???
             IT WAS ONLY A PECK!!! IT WAS
             SUPPOSED TO BE ON THE CHEEK!!! I
             ONLY GOT HIS LIPS BY MISTAKE!!!!
>
Iluvromance: Right. But didn't you go see
             Beauty and the Beast with J.P.
             last night?
>
FtLouie: Well, yes. But it was perfectly
             innocent. We just went as
             FRIENDS.
>

16

Iluvromance: But didn't you say in the past
that your ideal man is one who
can sit through an entire performance of *Beauty and the
Beast*, the most romantic and
beautiful story ever told, and
not snicker in the wrong places?
>
FtLouie: Yes. But that was a long time
ago. And I've realized since
then that I was wrong. Now my
ideal man is one who snickers.
>
Iluvromance: Well, you'd better tell Lilly
that.
>
FtLouie: Why? What's she saying? Wait a
minute - how does she even KNOW
what J.P. and I did last night?
How do YOU even know?
>
Iluvromance: Oh . . . you haven't seen it?
>
FtLouie: SEEN WHAT????
>
Iluvromance: The giant photo of you and J.P.
coming out of the theatre that's
in the *New York Post* this morning,
with the headline *Heartbroken
Princess Finds New Love*?

Heartbroken Princess
Finds New Love

It looks like splitsville for New York's own Princess Mia Thermopolis (of Genovia) and her long-time boyfriend, Columbia University student – and commoner – Michael Moscovitz.

Moscovitz is rumoured to have accepted a year-long appointment at a Japanese robotics firm in Tsukuba, where he'll be working on a top-secret project.

But Her Royal Highness doesn't appear to be pining for her one-time love – or wasting any time getting back into the dating scene. Her former beau has already been replaced by a mystery man who accompanied the young royal to a performance of the long-running Broadway show *Beauty and the Beast* last night. Undisclosed sources say that the young man is none other than John Paul Reynolds-Abernathy IV, son of the wealthy theatre promoter and producer John Paul Reynolds-Abernathy III.

A fellow theatre patron who observed the young couple in their private box asserted, 'They certainly seemed cosy up there,' while another stated, 'They make a very attractive couple. They're both so tall and blond.'

When asked for a statement, a Genovian Palace spokesman said, 'We do not comment on the Princess's personal life.'

Saturday, September 11, 10 a.m., the Loft

Well. At least now I know why I haven't heard from Lilly.

Which is so messed up on so many levels. I mean, first of all, it was only a peck.

And second of all, they were already broken up when the peck took place. And third of all, WE WENT TO THE SHOW AS FRIENDS. How could anyone in their right minds think I'm GOING OUT with J.P. Reynolds-Abernathy the Fourth?

I mean, sure, he's funny and cute and a nice guy and all. Don't get me wrong.

But my heart belongs to Michael Moscovitz, and always will!

None of this makes any sense. Lilly is supposed to be my best friend. How can she believe something so horrible of me?

And it's true, I *was* pretty awful to her brother this week. But that was only because I (stupidly) didn't realize what a great thing we had, until I went and lost it.

But I APOLOGIZED to him. It's only a matter of time (four hours) until he gets my email and calls me (please, God) and we patch things up and he sends me back my snowflake necklace and we're back together and everything's fine again.

Unless he happens to check Google News and sees the giant article about me and J.P.

But why would he *believe* it? He never believed any of the lies the paparazzi were always reporting about me and James Franco. Why would he believe THIS one?

He wouldn't. He *can't*.

So what is Lilly's *problem*?

Anyway. I am not going to freak out. It's true that in the past, I would have been hysterical over something like this. I'd be calling my dad and begging him to have our lawyers demand a retraction. I'd be trying to get to the bottom of who'd tipped the papers off – as if I didn't know (Grandmere). I'd be frantically e-ing Michael, hysterically explaining that none of it's true.

But not now. I'm way too mature for all that. Also, I'm used to it.

And besides: I am *way* too freaked out as it already is. How could I possibly freak out any *more*? I can barely hold on to my pen to write this, my hand is so drenched in sweat.

So . . . whatever. I'm going to allow Lilly a little cooling-off period. I'm sure when she's having her party and everyone is there but me (I called Tina after I ran out and got the paper. I told her that of COURSE she has to go to Lilly's party, even though she was going to boycott out of solidarity with me. But I actually *need* her to go so I can find out what Lilly is saying about me. I swear, if Lilly's bad-mouthing me, I will call the Federal Communications Commission and report the fact that she used the S word on last week's episode of *Lilly Tells It Like It Is*, while she was describing the current state of affairs in Iraq), she'll start missing me and call and invite me over.

And then I'll go and we'll hug it out and it will all be fine.

I'll just sit here and do my calculus homework until then. Because God knows I didn't pay much attention last week, so I have NO IDEA what's going on in that class. Or any of my classes really. The last thing I need, on top of everything else that's going on, is to flunk out of high school.

And I think while I'm doing that, I'll finish off the rest of the pork dumplings leftover from Number One Noodle Son (this meat thing is unreal. Once you start eating it, you really *can't* stop).

Because that's how a mature person would handle the situation.

FOUR HOURS TILL HE LANDS!!!!!!!

EEEEEEEEEEEEEEEEEEEEEEEEEEEEEEEEEEEEE
EEEEEEEEEEEEEEEEEEEEEEEEEEEEEEEEEEEEE
EEEEEEEEEEEEEEEEEEEEEEEEEEEEEEEEEEEEE
EEEEEEEEEEEEEEEEEEEEEEEEEEEEEEEEEEEEE
EEEEEEEEEEEEEEEEEEEEEEEEEEEEEEEEEEEEE
EEEEEEEEEEEEEEEEEEEEEEEEEEEEEEEEEEEEE
EEEEEEEEEEEEEEEEEEEEEEEEEEEEEEEEEEEEE
EEEEEEEEEEEEEEE

Saturday, September 11, 10.15 a.m., the Loft

So I just put my name in the Google News search engine to see how many stories there were about me, and what the likelihood of Michael seeing that piece about me and J.P. is and . . .

. . . there are 527 RSS articles about it.

And that's not all.

I went to Google Blog Search to see if anyone was blogging about me, and there's a new website up: www.ihatemiathermopolis.com.

There's a list there of the top-ten stupidest things about Mia Thermopolis.

Number one is my hair.

Number ten is my name.

The stuff in between gets progressively worse.

I know I'm supposed to ignore my negative press. Grandmere told me if I react to it or acknowledge it any way, I'm only feeding into it and giving the haters MORE to write about.

But this. This is really . . .

Great. Just great. Like I don't have ENOUGH to worry about.

Now somebody out there in the world hates me enough to point out for the whole world to read that, with my new haircut, my ears resemble teapot handles.

Great. Just what I need.

Saturday, September 11, 10.30 a.m., the Loft

Dear Michael

~~By now you've probably seen~~

Dear Michael

~~Hi! I was just wondering if you'd seen~~

Dear Michael

~~Whatever you do, don't look at~~

Dear Founder of ihatemiathermopolis.com

~~IF YOU HATE ME SO MUCH WHY DON'T YOU JUST TELL IT TO MY FACE, YOU COWARD????~~

Saturday, September 11, 2 p.m., the Loft

Inbox: 0

My cellphone just rang. I was so certain it was Michael (his plane has landed by now) that I almost dropped it, my hands were so sweaty and shaking so badly (also they were really greasy from the chicken leg I found in the back of the fridge and was gnawing).

But it was only J.P. He wanted to know if I'd seen the paper.

'Yes, isn't that funny?' I tried to sound all breezy. Which is hard to do with a leftover fried chicken leg in your mouth. 'They think we're in love. Ha ha.'

'Yeah,' J.P. said. 'Ha ha.'

I'm lucky he's such a good sport.

'I'm really sorry,' I said. 'It's sort of a hazard of hanging out with me. I mean, that you're going to end up in the paper.' I didn't mention ihatemiathermopolis.com. I figured he'd find out soon enough about that.

'I don't mind,' J.P. said. 'Being associated with a princess, the heir to a royal throne? And my parents are totally impressed. They think I've finally accomplished something.'

It was my turn to go, 'Ha ha.' Although the truth is I was feeling kind of sick. Maybe on account of all the meat I'd consumed in the past hour and a half. Basically everything that was in the fridge. I seriously don't know what's wrong with me. I've gone from a vegetarian to practically a cannibal in less than a week.

Well, OK, not a cannibal. But whatever you call an excessive meat eater.

Except that I knew the truth. My sick feeling had

nothing to do with all the meat I'd eaten, and everything to do with the fact that Michael's plane had totally landed, and that he'd conceivably be checking his messages at any minute.

'Listen,' J.P. said. 'I was wondering if you'd heard about Lilly's party.'

'Yeah,' I said. 'I'm not invited. Obviously.'

'I figured,' J.P. said with a sigh. 'I was hoping she'd gotten over that by now.'

'Well, seeing our pictures plastered all over the news together isn't going to help the situation any,' I said.

'No,' J.P. said. 'Maybe if we give her the weekend . . .'

'Maybe.' I hope so. But I don't really think the weekend is going to do it though.

'Want to get together and have a party of our own tonight?' J.P. asked. 'You know, show them how it's done?'

'Oh my gosh, that is so sweet of you,' I said. 'But I think I better stay here. Because Michael's plane has landed, so he should be checking his email soon. And I really want to be here when he calls.' *If* he calls.

But he has to call. *Right??????*

'Oh.' J.P. sounded kind of taken aback. 'Well, wouldn't it be better if you *weren't* there when he calls? So he realizes how sought after and popular you are?'

I laughed. J.P. really does have a twisted sense of humour.

'Funny! But I think there's a good chance he's going to realize that when he sees the paper. If that photo of us hits the AP wire, I mean, and makes it to Japan. Besides, I really do need to work on my calculus, if I'm going to pass.'

'Well, if you need help, I'll be happy to come over,'

J.P. offered. 'I'm a whizz at the summation of infinitesimal differences.'

Isn't he the sweetest? Imagine, offering to give up his Saturday to help me with calculus!

'Aw,' I said. 'That's so nice. But I'm good. I have an actual algebra instructor living here with me, who I can turn to if I start pulling out my hair in despair. I mean, what's left of my hair.'

'Well,' J.P. said. 'OK. But if you change your mind . . .'

'I'll know who to call,' I said. I was kind of trying to hurry him off the phone. Because Michael could have been calling at that very moment. Not that my cell wouldn't have told me. But. You know.

'OK,' J.P. said. 'Well, just remember. We make a "very attractive" couple.'

'Because we're both so tall and blond,' I said.

J.P. laughed too, and then hung up.

When the Yellowstone caldera last erupted, six hundred and forty thousand years ago, it released a thousand cubic kilometres in debris, basically covering half of North America in ash piles six feet deep.

This is totally what's going to happen when J.P. finally finds his one true love.

I know this is totally selfish to say, but I just hope that when he finds his, I still have mine.

Saturday, September 11, 4 p.m., the Loft

Inbox: 0
Calls: 0

I can't believe this. He hasn't e'd or called yet.

Mom just looked in here and went, 'Mia? Aren't you going out tonight?'

I guess she could tell by the fact that I'm wearing my Hello Kitty flannel pyjamas that I'm in for the night.

'Nah,' I said, managing to sound more carefree than I really feel. WHY HASN'T HE CALLED? 'I'm just going to hang here and catch up with my calculus homework.'

'Calculus homework?' Mom actually reached out and felt my forehead. 'You don't *feel* feverish . . .'

'Ha ha.' Everyone around me is turning into such a comedian lately. I totally put my hands behind my back so she couldn't see how sweaty they were.

'Mia,' Mom said, putting on her maternal face. 'You can't sit around in this apartment pining for Michael forever.'

'I know that,' I said, looking shocked. 'God, Mom! Do you think I'd do that? I'm a feminist, you know. I don't need a man to make me happy.' It's just, you know, when that particular one is around, and I smell his neck, my oxytocin levels rise, and I feel calmer and more relaxed than I do when I'm alone. Or with anyone else.

'Well.' Mom seemed sceptical. She knows about the oxytocin thing. 'I don't know. You're not staying in because of that silly news article then, are you?'

'You mean the one accusing me of dating my best

friend's ex-boyfriend when my own boyfriend and I have barely been broken up a week?' I asked lightly. 'Gee, no, why on earth would I let that bother me?'

'Mia.' Mom's lips started getting small, a sure sign she was unhappy with me. 'You can't let the fact that Michael is moving on with his life keep you from moving on with yours. Of course it's important to mourn the loss, but—'

'WHAT LOSS? MAYBE MICHAEL HASN'T GOTTEN MY APOLOGY EMAIL YET. FOR ALL WE KNOW, HE COULD BE OPENING HIS EMAIL RIGHT NOW AND SEEING THAT I APOLOGIZED AND BE GETTING READY TO CALL TO TAKE ME BACK. ANY SECOND NOW.'

'Stop yelling,' Mom said. 'Are you really feeling all right? You look a little peaked. Have you eaten anything today?'

'Um.' I wasn't sure how to break it to her that I'd polished off all the lunch meat and the Canadian bacon she'd been saving for breakfast. There wasn't a piece of meat left in the loft. Or any ice cream either. And I'd also finished all the Girl Scout Cookies. 'Yes.'

'Well, if you're sure you're feeling all right and you're going to stay here anyway,' Mom said, 'Frank and I might head on over to the Angelika to see that new grunge rockumentary. Would you mind watching Rocky while we're gone?'

'Sure,' I said. In lieu of smelling Michael's neck, I figured I could use a few hours of Rocky's favourite game, which involves pointing at various pieces in his Tonka collection and shouting the word, 'Tuck', which means *truck* in Rocky speak. It might relax me.

So now I'm here babysitting my brother.

If only the photographers from the *New York Post* could see me now. The glamorous life of America's favourite princess: sitting on the living-room floor with her baby brother, playing 'Tuck' in her flannel Hello Kitty pyjamas . . .

. . . while her heart slowly and irrevocably breaks.

Sunday, September 12, 10 a.m., the Loft

Inbox: 0
Calls: 0

But I have an instant message!!!

Oh, it's just from Tina. But I guess that's better than nothing.

```
Iluvromance: Hey, Mia!!!! Did he call?????
>
FtLouie:     Not yet. But I'm sure I'll hear
             soon. He's probably still getting
             settled and all that. He'll call
             or write as soon as he gets a
             chance.
```

God, I sound so brave and strong, when inwardly I'm quivering like a – I don't even know what – tiny quivering thing. WHY HASN'T HE CALLED????

```
Iluvromance: Of course he will. Unless he saw
             that photo, I mean.
```

OK, time to change the subject.

```
FtLouie:     So how was the party????
>
Iluvromance: The  party  was  OK,  I  guess.
             Nothing  too  exciting  happened.
             Kenny  Showalter  came  over  with  a
             bunch  of  guys  from  his  Muay  Thai
             fighting   class,   and   they   all
```

started doing shirtless handstand push-ups, and I guess Lilly was impressed by what she saw since she totally hooked up with one of them. And then Perin ate too many maraschino cherries and threw up in the bathroom sink, and a lot of the cherries were still whole so Ling Su had to cut them up with scissors to get them to go down the drain. That's about it. Like I said, you didn't miss much.

>

FtLouie: Wait a minute. Lilly HOOKED UP with a GUY FROM KENNY SHOW-ALTER'S MUAY THAI FIGHTING CLASS?

>

Iluvromance: Oh. Yeah. Well, I mean, Boris said he saw Lilly making out with some dude in the kitchen. But she threw a lobster-pot holder at his head before he could get a good look at who it was. You know Boris is afraid of lobsters—

>

FtLouie: But it was definitely one of the Muay Thai fighters????

>

Iluvromance: Yeah. Well, the guy wasn't wearing a shirt, so it had to be.

```
>
FtLouie:      But that's just . . . that's so
              wrong! I mean, she hasn't even
              had a chance to recover from her
              heartbreak over J.P.! This is
              obviously just a rebound rela-
              tionship! What does Lilly think
              she's doing? Someone's got to
              talk to her. Did you try talking
              to her????
>
Iluvromance: Well . . . sort of. But she just
              laughed in my face and told me
              not to be such a—
>
FtLouie:      Such a what? Such a WHAT?
>
Iluvromance: Nothing. Mia, I have to go, my
              mom's calling me. TTYL!
```

But the thing was, she didn't have to say it. I know what Lilly told her.

Not to be such a Mia.

But there's a REASON I worry so much about her. Sometimes Lilly makes really bad choices. And then she gets hurt.

And true, sometimes she makes good choices – like dating J.P. – and gets hurt anyway.

But making out with some random Muay Thai fighter in her kitchen just one day after breaking up with her boyfriend of six months?

I don't see how that can be a good choice.

Someone's got to talk to her before she does something she regrets.

If Dr Moscovitz didn't completely hate me right now – for dumping her son and then ALLEGEDLY dating her daughter's boyfriend – I'd call her.

But given the current state of our relationship, that is probably not the wisest course of action.

Sunday, September 12, 11 a.m., the Loft

Inbox: 0
Calls: . . .

But then my cell rang!
 But it wasn't Michael. It was just J.P.

J.P.: 'Hey! How are you?'

It was kind of hard to hide my crushing disappointment.

Me: 'Fine. You?'

J.P.: 'What's wrong? Wait – don't tell me he hasn't called.'

Me: 'He hasn't called.'

Unintelligible muttering from his end of the phone. Then:

J.P.: 'Don't worry. He'll call.'

Me: 'I hope so.'

J.P.: 'Are you kidding? He'd be a fool not to. So how was your night last night?'

Me: 'Fine. I mean, I didn't do much. Just played Tuck with my brother.'

J.P.: 'You played WHAT?'

See, Michael knows what Tuck is. Not only that, he's PLAYED it with Rocky. I think he even LIKES playing it. It relaxes him as much as it relaxes me.

Me: 'It's – never mind. Did you hear about Lilly?'

J.P.: 'No. What about her?'

I didn't want to be the bearer of bad news about J.P.'s ex, but I figured it was better he heard it from me than from someone in school on Monday.

Me: 'She hooked up with some random Muay Thai fighter at her party last night.'

Instead of the inhalation of horror I expected to hear, however, J.P. sounded . . . well, almost as if he was *laughing*.

J.P.: 'That sounds like Lilly all right.'

I was shocked. I mean, sure, it sounded like the OLD Lilly – the pre-J.P. Lilly. But not the new-and-improved Lilly.
And he was *laughing!*

Me: 'J.P., don't you see? Lilly's just acting out because she's so crushed and broken-hearted over what she perceives as our betrayal of her! This whole Muay Thai fighter thing is directly related to that *New York Post* cover. We've got to do something before she descends into an ever-increasing downward spiral of self-destructive behaviour, like Lindsay Lohan!'

J.P.: 'Well, I don't see what we can do. Lilly's pretty much old enough to make her own decisions. If she wants to hook up with random Muay Thai fighters, that's really her business, not ours.'

I couldn't believe he was still *laughing*.

Me: 'J.P. It's not funny.'

J.P.: 'Well, it kinda is.'

Me: 'No, it's not, it's—'

Sunday, September 12, Noon, the Loft

I had to stop writing just then because my cellphone rang again. It was Michael.

He's in Japan. He got my email.

He also saw the picture of J.P. and me on the cover of the *New York Post*.

He said that it didn't make any difference though. He said he was sorry that we have to do this over the phone, but that there was no other way.

I asked him what he meant by 'this', and he said he'd been thinking about it the whole way to Japan, and that he really feels it would be better if he and I just went back to being what we used to be before we started going out – friends.

He said that he thought we both probably had some growing up to do, and that maybe some time apart – and seeing other people – would do us good.

I said OK. Even though every word he was saying was like a stab wound to my heart.

And then I said goodbye and hung up. Because I was afraid he would hear me sobbing.

And that isn't how I want him to remember me.

Sunday, September 12, 12.30 p.m., the Loft

WHY DID I SAY OK??????????????????
    Why didn't I say what I really felt, that I understand the part about having some growing up to do and spending some time apart . . .
    . . . but not the part about just being friends and seeing other people????
    Why didn't I say what I was thinking, which is that I'd rather DIE than be with anybody but him?????
    Why didn't I tell him the truth?????

And I KNOW it wouldn't have made any difference, and I just would have come across as exactly what he thinks I am – an immature little girl.

But at least he wouldn't think I'm OK with this.

Because I am NOT OK with this.

I will NEVER be OK with this.

I don't think I will ever be OK again.

Monday, September 13, 8 a.m., the Loft

Mom came into my room just now to say she understands that I'm grieving about having lost the love of my life.

She said she understands how upsetting it must have been to me to have experienced such a hideous breakup as well as the loss of my best friend in one week.

She said she completely sympathizes with my plight, and appreciates that I feel the need to mourn my loss.

She said she has tried to give me the time and freedom I need in order to grieve.

But she said a whole day in bed is long enough.

Also that she's sick of seeing me in my Hello Kitty flannel pyjamas, which, if she isn't mistaken, I haven't changed out of since Saturday. Also that it's time to get up, get dressed, and go to school.

Of course I had no choice but to tell her the truth:

That I am dying.

Of course I know I'm not really dying.

But why does it feel that way?

I keep hoping it will all just . . . go away.

But it won't. It doesn't. I keep hoping when I close my eyes and go to sleep, that when I open them again it will have all been a terrible nightmare.

Only it never is. Every time I wake up, I'm still in my Hello Kitty pyjamas – the same ones I was wearing when Michael said he thought we should just go back to being friends – and WE'RE STILL BROKEN UP.

Mom told me I'm not dying. Even after I had her feel my clammy palms and erratic pulse. Even when I showed her the whites of my eyes, which have gone noticeably yellow. Even when I showed her my tongue, which is basically white instead of a healthy pink. Even when I informed her that I went to wrongdiagnosis.com, and that it's obvious I have meningitis.

In which case, Mom said, I had better get dressed so she could take me to the emergency room.

I knew then she'd called my bluff. So I just begged her to let me stay in bed for one more day. And she finally relented.

I didn't tell her the truth: that I am never getting out of bed again.

It's true. I mean, think about it: now that Michael's gone from my life, there's no actual *reason* for me to get out of bed. Such as, for instance, to go to school.

It's true. I am the Princess of Genovia. But I will ALWAYS be the Princess of Genovia, whether I go to school or not.

So what does it matter if I go to school? I'm always going to have a job – Princess of Genovia – whether I graduate from high school or not.

And, since I'm sixteen now, no one can FORCE me to go to school.

Therefore, I've decided I'm not going. Ever again.

Mom said she'll call the school and tell them I won't be coming in today, and that she'll call Grandmere and tell her I won't be able to make it to princess lessons this afternoon either. She even said she'd tell Lars he has the day off, and that I can spend one more day wallowing in my bed if I want to.

But that tomorrow, no matter what I say, I'm going to school.

To which all I have to say is, that's what SHE thinks.

Maybe Dad will let me move to Genovia.

Monday, September 13, 5 p.m., the Loft

Tina just stopped by. Mom let her in to see me.

I really wish she hadn't.

I guess the fact that I haven't bathed in two days must show, since Tina's eyes got very wide when she saw me.

Still, she pretended like she wasn't shocked by the amount of grease in my hair or anything. She went, 'Your mom told me. About Michael. Mia, I'm so sorry. When are you coming back to school? Everyone misses you!'

'Lilly doesn't,' I said.

'Well,' Tina said, wincing. 'No, that's true. But still. You can't stay shut up in your room for the rest of your life, Mia.'

'I know,' I said. 'I'll be back in school tomorrow.' But this was a total lie. Even as I said it, I could feel my palms getting sweaty. Just the thought of going to school made me want to hurl.

'I'm so glad,' Tina said. 'I know things didn't work out with Michael, but maybe that's for the best. I mean, he's so much older than you are, and you two are in such different places in your lives, you still in high school, and him in college and all.'

I couldn't believe it. Even Tina – always my staunchest supporter where my love for Michael is concerned – was betraying me. I tried not to let my shock at this show, however.

'Besides,' Tina went on, blithely unaware of the pain she was causing me, 'now you can really concentrate on writing that novel you've always wanted to write. And you can work harder at school and your grades and get into a really great college, where you'll meet a really great guy who will make you forget all about Michael!'

Yeah. Because that's what I want to do. Forget all about Michael. The only guy – the only PERSON – I've ever felt completely calm around.

I didn't say that though. Instead, I said, 'You know what, Tina? You're right. I'll see you at school tomorrow. I promise.'

And Tina went away all happy, thinking she'd cheered me up.

But I don't actually believe that. You know, that anything Tina said is true.

And I'm not really going to school tomorrow. I just said it to get Tina to go away. Because having to talk to her made me feel so tired. I just wanted to go back to sleep.

In fact, that is what I'm going to do now. Writing all this has totally exhausted me.

Just *living* exhausts me.

Maybe this time, when I wake up, it really will all turn out to have been a bad dream . . .

Tuesday, September 14, 8 a.m., the Loft

No such luck, with the bad dream thing. I could tell by the way Mr Gianini came in here with a steaming mug of hot chocolate, going, 'Rise and shine, Mia! Look what I've got! Hot cocoa! With whipped cream! But you can only have it if you get out of bed, get dressed and get in the limo for school.'

He'd never have done that if I hadn't been brutally dumped by my long-time boyfriend, and currently in the throes of despair.

Poor Mr G. I mean, you have to give him points for trying. You really do.

I said I didn't want any hot cocoa. Then I explained – very politely – that I am not going to school. Any more.

I checked my tongue in the mirror just now. It's not as white as it was yesterday. It's possible I don't have meningitis after all.

But what else can explain the fact that whenever I think about how Michael isn't in my life any more, my heart starts beating very fast and won't slow down again for sixty seconds, or sometimes even longer?

Unless I have Lassa fever. But I've never even been to West Africa.

Tuesday, September 14, 5 p.m., the Loft

Tina came by again after school today. This time she had all my homework assignments that I've missed with her.

Also, Boris.

Boris was a little surprised to see me in my current condition. I know because he said so. He said, 'Mia, it is very surprising to me that a feminist like yourself would be so upset over the fact that a man had rejected her.'

Then he said, 'Ooof!' because Tina elbowed him so hard in the ribs.

He didn't believe my Lassa fever story.

So then, even though I really don't want to hurt anyone – because God knows I myself am in enough pain for everyone – I was forced to remind Boris that back when a certain ex-girlfriend of his had rejected him, he'd dropped an entire globe on his head in a misguided attempt to get her back. I said that in comparison, me refusing to bathe or get out of bed for a few days was really nothing.

To which he agreed. Although he did keep sniffing the air in my bedroom and going, 'May I open a window? It seems a little . . . warm in here.'

I don't care that I smell. The truth is, I don't care about anything. Isn't that sad?

This made it hard for Tina to engage me in mindless conversation, something I can tell she'd been charged with doing, no doubt by my mother. Tina tried to get me interested in going back to school by telling me that both J.P. and Kenny had been asking about me . . . particularly J.P., who'd given Tina something to give to me – a tightly folded note that I had zero interest in reading.

After what seemed like forever – I know! It's pretty sad when even one of your best friends' attempts to cheer you up falls flat – Tina and Boris finally went away. I opened the note J.P. gave Tina to give to me. It said a lot of stuff, like, *Come on, it can't be THAT bad.* And *Why won't you return any of my calls?* and *I'll take you to see* Tarzan*! Orchestra seats!* and *Just come back to school. I miss you.*

Which was totally sweet of him.

But when your life is crumbling apart around you, the last place in the world you want to be is school . . . no matter how many cute guys there say they miss you.

Wednesday, September 15, 8 a.m., the Loft

Mom came bursting in here this morning, her mouth practically invisible, she had her lips pressed together so tightly. She said she gets that I'm sad. She said she gets that I feel like there's no point in living because my boyfriend dumped me, my best friend isn't speaking to me and I have no choice over what career I'm going to have some day. She says she gets that my palms won't stop sweating, I have heart palpitations and my tongue is a funny colour.

But then she said that three days of wallowing is her limit. She said I was getting up and getting dressed and going to school if she had to drag me to the shower and stick me under the nozzle herself.

I just stayed exactly where I've been for the past sixty-eight hours – my bed – and looked at her without saying anything. I couldn't believe she could be so cold. I mean, really.

Then she tried a different tactic. She started to cry. She said she's really worried about me and that she doesn't know what to do. She says she's never seen me this way – that I didn't even do anything the other day when Rocky tried to stick a dime up his nose. She said a week ago I'd have been freaking out over loose change around the house being a choking hazard.

Now I didn't even care.

Which isn't true. I *don't* want Rocky to choke. And I *don't* want to make my mother cry.

But at the same time, I don't see what I can do to keep either of these things from happening.

Then Mom switched tack again, and stopped crying, and asked if I wanted her to bring out the big guns. She said that she doesn't want to bother Dad while he's busy with the United Nations General Assembly, but that I really wasn't leaving her much choice. Was that what I wanted her to do? To bother my dad with this?

I told her she could call Dad if she wanted to. I told her that actually I'd been meaning to talk to Dad anyway about moving to Genovia full time. Because the truth is – I don't want to live in Manhattan any more.

All I wanted was for Mom to leave me alone so I could continue feeling sorry for myself in peace. My plan actually worked . . . a little *too* well. She got so upset, she ran out of my room crying.

I really didn't mean to make her cry! I'm sorry to have made her feel bad. Especially because I don't really want to move to Genovia. I'm sure they won't let me lounge around in bed all day there. Which I'm really sort of starting to like doing. I have a whole little schedule now. Every morning, I get up before anyone else does and have breakfast – usually whatever leftovers are in the fridge from the evening meal the night before – and feed Fat Louie and clean out his box.

Then I get back into bed, and eventually Fat Louie joins me, and together we watch the top-ten video countdown on MTV, and then the one on VH1. Then, when either Mom or Mr G comes in and tries to get me to go to school, I say no . . . which usually exhausts me so much I have to take a little nap for a while.

Then I wake up in time to watch *The View* and two back-to-back episodes of *Judging Amy*.

Then, after I make sure no one else is around, I go out into the kitchen and have some lunch – a ham sandwich or microwave popcorn or something. It doesn't matter much what – and then get back into bed with

Fat Louie and watch Judge Milian on *The People's Court*, and then *Judge Judy*.

Then my mom sends in Tina, and I pretend to be alive, and then Tina leaves, and I go to sleep, because Tina exhausts me. Then, after Mom and everybody are asleep, I get up, make myself a snack, and watch TV until two or three in the morning.

Then I get up a few hours later and do it all over again, after I realize I wasn't actually dreaming and I really am truly broken up with Michael.

I could conceivably keep this up until I'm eighteen, and start receiving my yearly salary as Princess of Genovia (which doesn't kick in until I'm a legal adult and begin my official duties as heir).

And, OK, it's going to be hard to do my official duties from bed.

But I bet I could figure out a way.

Still. It sucks to make your mother cry. Maybe I should make her a card or something.

Except that would involve getting out of bed to look for markers and stuff. And I am way, way too tired to do all that.

Wednesday, September 15, 5 p.m., the Loft

I guess my mom wasn't kidding about bringing out the big guns. Tina didn't show up after school today.

Grandmere did.

But – much as I love her, and sorry as I am to have made her cry – Mom's totally wrong if she thinks anything Grandmere says or does is going to change my mind about going back to school.

I'm not doing it. There's just no point.

'What do you mean, there's no point?' Grandmere wanted to know when I said this. 'Of course there's a point. You have to *learn*.'

'Why?' I asked her. 'My future job is totally assured. Throughout the ages, most reigning monarchs have been total morons, and yet they still were allowed to rule. What difference does it make whether I've graduated from high school or not?'

'Well, you don't want to be an ignoramus,' Grandmere insisted. She was perched on the very edge of my bed, holding her purse in her lap and looking around all askance at everything, like the homework assignments Tina had left the day before and that I'd sort of thrown across the floor, and my *Buffy the Vampire Slayer* action figures, apparently not realizing they are expensive collectables now, like her stupid Limoges teacups.

But from Grandmere's expression, you could tell that, instead of being in her teenage granddaughter's bedroom, she felt like she was in some back-alley pawnshop in Chinatown or something.

And OK, I guess it *is* pretty messy in here. But whatever.

'Why don't I want to be an ignoramus?' I asked. 'Some of the most influential women on the planet didn't graduate from high school either.'

'Name one,' Grandmere demanded with a snort.

'Paris Hilton,' I said. 'Lindsay Lohan. Nicole Richie.'

'I am quite certain,' Grandmere said, 'that all those women graduated from high school. And even if they didn't, it's nothing to be proud of. Ignorance is never attractive. Speaking of which, how long has it been since you washed your hair, Amelia?'

But I fail to see the point in bathing. What does it matter how I look now that Michael is out of my life?

When I mentioned this, however, Grandmere asked if I was feeling all right.

'No, I'm not, Grandmere,' I said. 'Which I would have thought was obvious by the fact that I haven't gotten out of my bed in three days except to eat and go to the bathroom.'

'Oh, Amelia,' Grandmere said, looking offended. 'We've stooped to scatological references now, as well? *Really*. I understand you're sad about losing That Boy, but—'

'Grandmere,' I said. 'I think you'd better go now.'

'I won't go until we've decided what we're going to do about *this*.'

And then Grandmere tapped on the Domina Rei stationery from Mrs Weinberger, which she'd found peeping out from beneath my bed.

'Oh, that,' I said. 'Please have your secretary decline for me.'

'Decline?' Grandmere's drawn-on eyebrows lifted. 'We shall do no such thing, young lady. Do you have any idea what Elana Trevanni said when I ran into her at

Bergdorf's yesterday and casually mentioned to her that my granddaughter had been invited to speak at the Domina Rei's charity gala? She said—'

'Fine,' I interrupted again. 'I'll do it.'

Grandmere didn't say anything for a beat. Then she asked hesitantly, 'Did you just say you'll do it, Amelia?'

'Yes,' I said. Anything to make her go away. 'I'll do it. Just . . . can we talk about it later? I have a headache.'

'You're probably dehydrated,' Grandmere said. 'Have you drunk your eight glasses of water today? You know you need to drink eight glasses of water a day, Amelia, in order to keep hydrated. That's how we Renaldo women preserve our dewy complexions, by consuming plenty of liquids . . .'

'I think I just need to rest,' I said in a weak voice. 'My throat is starting to hurt a little. I don't want to get laryngitis and lose my voice before the big event . . . it's a week from Friday, right?'

'Good heavens,' Grandmere said, leaping up from my bed so quickly that she startled Fat Louie from the pillow fort I'd made him at my side. He was nothing but an orange blur as he ran for the safety of the closet. 'We can't have you coming down with something that might endanger your attending the gala! I shall send over my personal physician immediately!'

She started fumbling in her purse for her bejewelled cellphone – which she only knows how to work because I showed her about a million times – but I stopped her by saying weakly, 'No, it's all right, Grandmere. I think I just need to rest . . . you'd better go. Whatever I have, you don't want to catch it . . .'

Grandmere was out of there like a shot.

And FINALLY I could go back to sleep.

Or so I thought. Because a few minutes later, Mom came into the doorway and stood there peering down at me with a troubled look on her face.

'Mia,' she said. 'Did you tell your grandmother you'd speak at a Domina Rei Women's Society benefit?'

'Yeah,' I said, pulling my pillow over my head. 'Anything, to make her leave me alone . . .'

Mom went away, looking concerned.

I don't know what *she's* so worried about. *I'm* the one who's going to have to find some way to get out of town before the event actually happens.

Thursday, September 16, 11 a.m., Dad's Limo

This morning at nine o'clock I was in bed with my eyes squeezed shut (because I heard someone coming and I didn't want to deal) when my covers were thrown back and this stern, deep voice said, 'Get. Up.'

I opened my eyes and was surprised to see my dad standing there, wearing his business suit and smelling of autumn.

I've been inside so long, I've forgotten what outside smells like.

I could tell by his expression that I was in for it.

So I said, 'No,' and snatched the covers back, pulling them over my head.

Which is when I heard my dad go, 'Lars. If you will.'

And then my bodyguard scooped me – covers still clutched over my head – from my bed, and began to carry me from my mother's apartment.

'What are you doing?' I demanded, when I had disentangled my head from the covers, and saw that we were in the hallway, and that Ronnie, our neighbour, was blinking at us in astonishment with her arms full of grocery bags.

'Something that's for your own good,' my dad said from behind Lars, on the stairs.

'But.' I seriously couldn't believe this. 'I'm in my pyjamas!'

'I told you to get up,' Dad said. 'You're the one who wouldn't do it.'

'You can't do this to me!' I cried, as we exited the apartment building and headed towards my dad's limo. 'I'm an American! I have rights, you know!'

My dad looked at me very sarcastically and said, 'No, you don't. You're a teenager.'

'Help!' I screamed to all the New York University students who live in our neighbourhood and were just rolling home after a fun night out in the East Village. 'Call Amnesty International! I'm being held against my will!'

'Lars,' my dad said disgustedly as the NYU kids looked around for the movie cameras they evidently thought were rolling, since the whole thing appeared to be some scene from a *Law & Order* episode being filmed on Thompson Street or something. 'Toss her in the car.'

And Lars did! He tossed me in the car!

And OK, he tossed my journal in after me. And a pen.

And my Chinese slippers with the sequin flowers on the toes.

But still! Is this any way to treat a princess, I ask you? Or even a human being?

And Dad won't tell me where we're going. He just goes, 'You'll see,' when I ask.

After getting over the initial shock of being man-handled in such a way, I find, to my surprise, that I don't much care. I mean, it's weird to be sitting in my dad's limo in my Hello Kitty pyjamas, with my sheet and duvet wrapped around me.

But at the same time, I can't summon up any real indignation about it.

I think that might actually be the problem. That I just don't care about *anything* any more.

Except I can't even be bothered to care about *that* very much either.

Thursday, September 16, Noon, Dr Knutz's Office

We're sitting in a *psychologist's* office.

I'm not even kidding. My dad didn't take me to the royal jet to go back to Genovia. He brought me to the Upper East Side to see a *psychologist*.

And not just any psychologist either. One of the nation's pre-eminent experts in adolescent and child psychology. At least if all the many degrees and awards framed on the wall of his outer office is any indication.

I guess this is supposed to impress me. Or at least comfort me.

Although I can't say I feel too comforted by the fact that his name is Dr Arthur T. *Knutz*.

Yes, that's right. My dad has brought me to see Dr Knutz. Because he – and Mom and Mr G – apparently thinks *I'm* nuts.

I know I probably *look* nuts, sitting here in my pyjamas with my duvet still clutched around me. But whose fault is that? They could have let me get dressed.

Not that I *would* have, of course. But if they'd told me they were taking me out of the apartment, I might have at least put on a bra.

Dr Knutz's receptionist – or nurse or whatever she is – doesn't seem too bothered by my mode of dress, however. She just went, 'Good morning, Prince Philippe,' to my dad when he brought me in. Well, I mean, when Lars carried me in. Because when the limo pulled up in front of the brownstone Dr Knutz's office is in, I wouldn't get out of the car. I wasn't going to walk across East 78th Street in my Hello Kitty pyjamas! I may be crazy, but I'm not THAT crazy.

So Lars carried me.

The receptionist didn't seem to think it was at all weird that her boss's newest patient had to be carried in to his office. She just went, 'Dr Knutz will be with you in a moment. In the meantime, will you please fill this out, dear?'

I don't know why I got so panicky all of a sudden. But I was like, 'No. What is it? A test? I don't want to take a test.' It's weird, but my heart started beating all crazy at the idea of having to take a test.

The receptionist just looked at me all funny and went, 'It's just an assessment of how you're feeling. There are no right or wrong answers. It will only take a minute to fill out.'

But I didn't want to take an assessment, even if there were no right or wrong answers.

'No,' I said. 'I don't think so.'

'Here,' Dad said, and held out his hand to the receptionist. 'I'll take one too. Will that make you feel better, Mia?'

For some reason, it did. Because, to be honest, if I'm crazy, so is my dad. I mean, you should see how many shoes he owns. And he's a *man*.

So the receptionist handed my dad the same form to fill out that she handed me. When I looked down, I saw that it was a list of statements that you were supposed to rate by checking off the most appropriate answer. Statements like, *I feel like there's no point in living*. To which you could check off one of the following replies:

All the time
Most of the time
Some of the time

A little of the time
None of the time

Since there was nothing else to do and I had a pen in my hand anyway, I filled out the form. I noticed when I was done that I had checked off mainly *All the time* and *Most of the time*. Such as, *I feel like everyone hates me . . . Most of the time* and *I feel that I am worthless . . . Most of the time*.

But my dad had filled out mainly *A little of the time* and *None of the time*.

Even for his answers to statements like, *I feel as if true romantic love has passed me by*.

Which I happen to know is a total lie. Dad told me he has only ever had one true love in his entire life, and that was Mom, and that he let her go and totally regretted it. That's why he urged me not to be stupid and let Michael go. Because he knew I might never find a love like that again.

Too bad I didn't figure out he was right until it was too late.

Still, it's easy for him to feel like everyone hates him none of the time. There's no ihateprincephilippeof-genovia.com.

The receptionist – Mrs Hopkins – just collected our forms and took them through a door to the right of her desk. I couldn't see what was behind the door. Meanwhile, Lars picked up the latest copy of *Sports Illustrated* from Dr Knutz's waiting-room coffee table and started reading it all casually, like he carries princesses in their pyjamas into psychologists' offices every day of the week.

I bet he never thought that was going to be part of

his job description when he graduated from bodyguard school.

'I think you're going to like Dr Knutz, Mia,' my dad is saying. 'I met him at a fund-raising event last year. He's one of the nation's pre-eminent experts in adolescent and child psychology.'

I point at the awards on the wall. 'Yeah. I got that part.'

'Well,' Dad says. 'It's true. He comes very highly recommended. Don't let his name – or his demeanour – fool you.'

His demeanour? What does *that* mean?

Mrs Hopkins is back. She says the doctor will see us now.

Great.

Thursday, September 16, 2 p.m., Dad's Limo

Well. That was the weirdest thing. Ever.

Dr Knutz was . . . not what I was expecting.

I don't know what I was expecting really, but not Dr Knutz. I know Dad said not to let his name or his demeanour fool me, but I mean, from his name and his profession I expected him to be a little old bald dude with a goatee and glasses and maybe a German accent.

And he *was* old. Like Grandmere's age.

But he wasn't little. And he wasn't bald. And he didn't have a goatee. And he had sort of a Western accent. That's because, he explained, when he isn't at his practice in New York City, he's at his ranch in Montana.

Yes. That's right. Dr Knutz is a cowboy. A *cowboy* psychologist.

It so figures that out of all the psychologists in New York, I would end up with a cowboy one.

His office is furnished like the inside of a ranch house. There are pictures of wild mustangs running free on the wood panelling along his office walls. And every one of the books on the shelves behind him are by the famous Western authors Louis L'Amour and Zane Grey. His office furniture is dark leather and trimmed with brass studs. There's even a cowboy hat hanging on the peg on the back of the door. And the carpet is a Navajo rug.

I could tell right away from all this that Dr Knutz certainly lived up to his name. Also, that he was way crazier than me.

This had to be a joke. My dad had to be kidding that Dr Knutz is one of the nation's pre-eminent experts in adolescent and child psychology. Maybe I was being *Punk'd*. Maybe Ashton Kutcher was going to pop out any minute and be all, 'D'oh! Princess Mia! You're just been *Punk'd*! This guy isn't a psychologist at all! He's my Uncle Joe!'

'So,' Dr Knutz said, in this big booming cowboy voice after I'd sat down next to Dad on the couch across from Dr Knutz's big leather armchair. 'You're Princess Mia. Nice to meetcha. Heard you were uncharacteristically nice to your grandma yesterday.'

I was completely shocked by this. Unlike Dr Knutz's other patients, who, presumably, are children, I happen to be acquainted with a pair of Jungian psychologists – Dr and Dr Moscovitz – so I am not unfamiliar with how doctor–patient relationships are supposed to go.

And they are not supposed to begin with completely false accusations on the part of the doctor.

'That is total and utter libel,' I said. 'I wasn't nice to her. I just said what she wanted to hear so she would go away.'

'Oh,' Dr Knutz said. 'That's different. So you're telling me everything is hunky-dory then?'

'Obviously not,' I said. 'Since I am sitting here in your office in my pyjamas and a duvet.'

'You know, I'd noticed that,' Dr Knutz said. 'But you young girls are always wearing the oddest things, so I just figured it was the new fashion craze or something.'

I could see right away that this was never going to fly. How could I entrust my innermost emotional thoughts to someone who goes around calling me and my peers 'you young girls' and thinks any of us would willingly go outside dressed in Hello Kitty pyjamas and a duvet?

'This isn't going to work for me,' I said to my dad as I got up. 'Let's go.'

'Hang on a second, Mia,' Dad said. 'We just got here, OK? Give the man a chance.'

'Dad,' I couldn't believe this. I mean, if I had to go to therapy, why couldn't my parents have found me a *real* therapist, not a COWBOY therapist? 'Let's go. Before he BRANDS me.'

'You got something against ranchers, little lady?' Dr Knutz wanted to know.

'Um, considering that I'm a vegetarian,' I said – I didn't mention that I stopped being a vegetarian a week ago – 'yes, yes, I do.'

'You seem awful hetted up,' Dr Knutz said. I swear he really said *hetted* and not *heated*. 'For someone who according to this says she finds herself not caring about anything at all most of the time.'

He tapped the assessment sheet I'd filled out in his outer office. Sinking back down in my seat, since I could tell this was going to take a while, I said, 'Look, Doctor, um –' I couldn't even bring myself to say his name! 'I think you should know that I've been studying the work of Dr Carl Jung for some time. I have been struggling to achieve self-actualization for years. I am no stranger to psychology. I happen to know perfectly well what's wrong with me.'

'Oh, you do,' Dr Knutz said, looking intrigued. 'Enlighten me.'

'I'm just,' I said, 'feeling a little down. It's a normal reaction to something that happened to me last week.'

'Right,' Dr Knutz said, looking down at a piece of paper on his desk. 'You broke up with your boyfriend – Michael, is it?'

'Yes,' I said. 'And, OK, maybe it's a little more complicated than a normal teenagers' break-up, because I'm a princess and Michael is a genius, and he thinks he has to go off to Japan to build a robotic surgical arm in order to prove to my family that he's worthy of me, when the truth is, *I'm* not worthy of *him*, and I suppose because deep down inside I know that, I completely sabotaged our relationship.

'And, OK, maybe we were doomed from the start, because I scored an INFJ on the Myers-Briggs Jungian personality test we took online last summer, and he scored an ENTJ, and now he just wants to be friends and see other people, which is the *last* thing I want. But I respect his wishes, and I know that if I ever hope to attain the fruits of self-actualization, I have to spend more time building up the roots of my tree of life, and . . . and . . . and, really, that's it. Except for possible meningitis. Or Lassa fever. That's all that's wrong with me. I just have to adjust. I'm fine. I'm really fine.'

'You're fine?' Dr Knutz said. 'You've missed almost a week of school even though there's nothing physically wrong with you – we'll check on the meningitis of course – and you haven't changed out of your pyjamas in days. But you're fine.'

'Yes,' I said. Suddenly I was very close to tears. Also, my heart was beating kind of fast again. 'Can I go home now?'

'Why?' Dr Knutz wanted to know. 'So you can crawl back into bed and continue to isolate yourself from friends and loved ones – a classic sign of depression, by the way?'

I just blinked at him. I couldn't believe he – a perfect stranger. WORSE, a stranger who likes WESTERN

THINGS – was talking to me that way. Who did he think he was anyway – one of the nation's pre-eminent experts in adolescent and child psychology aside?

'So you can continue to drift away from your long-term relationship with your best friend, Lilly,' he said, referring to a note on the pad in his lap, 'as well as your other friends, by avoiding school and any other social settings where you might be forced to interact with them?'

I blinked at him some more. I know *I* was supposed to be the crazy one, but it was hard to believe from this statement that *he* wasn't crazy.

I was *not* avoiding school because I might have to see Lilly there, or interact socially with people. That wasn't it at *all*. Or why I want to move to Genovia.

'So you can continue to ignore the things you used to love – like Instant Messaging your friend Tina – and sleep during the day, then stay up all night,' Dr Knutz went on, 'gaining weight through compulsive binge eating when you think no one is looking?'

Wait . . . how did he know about THAT? HOW DID HE KNOW ABOUT TINA? OR THE GIRL SCOUT COOKIES?

'So you can go on just saying whatever it is you think people want to hear in order to make them go away and leave you alone, and refusing to observe even basic proper hygiene – again, classic examples of adolescent depression?'

I just rolled my eyes. Because everything he was saying is totally ridiculous. I'm not depressed. I'm *sad*, maybe. Because everything sucks. And I probably *do* have meningitis, even though everyone seems to be ignoring my symptoms.

But I'm not depressed.

'So you can continue to cut yourself off from the things you used to love – your baby brother, your parents, your school activities, your friends – and go on feeling consumed by self-loathing, yet lacking any motivation to change, or enjoy life again?' Dr Knutz's voice boomed very loudly in his ranch-style office. 'I could go on. Do I need to?'

I blinked at him some more. Only now I was blinking back tears. I couldn't believe it. I really couldn't.

I don't have meningitis. I don't have Lassa fever.

I'm depressed. I'm actually *depressed*.

'I might,' I said, after clearing my throat, because it was kind of hard to talk around the big lump that had suddenly appeared there, 'be a little down.'

'You know, there's nothing wrong with admitting you're depressed,' Dr Knutz went on in a gentle voice. I mean, for a cowboy. 'Many, many people have suffered from depression. Having depression doesn't mean you're crazy, or a failure, or a bad person.'

I had to blink back a lot of tears.

'OK,' was all I could manage to say.

Then my dad reached over and took my hand. Which I didn't really appreciate, because that just made me want to cry more. Plus, my hand was super sweaty.

'And it's OK to cry,' Dr Knutz went on, passing me a box of tissues he'd had hidden somewhere.

How did he keep doing that? How did he keep reading my mind? Was it because he spent so much time out on the range? With the deer? And the antelope? What *is* an antelope anyway?

'It's perfectly normal, and even healthy, considering what's been going on in your life lately, Mia, that you might feel sad and need to talk to someone about it,' Dr Knutz was saying. 'That's why your family brought you here to see me. But unless you yourself admit that you have a problem and need help, there's very little I can do. So why don't you say what's *really* bothering you, and how you're *really* feeling? And this time, leave the Jungian tree of self-actualization out of it.'

And then – before I knew what was happening – I found myself not even caring that I was possibly being *Punk'd*.

Maybe it was the Navajo rug. Maybe it was the cowboy hat on the peg on the back of the door. Maybe I just figured he was right: I couldn't really spend the rest of my life in my room.

In any case, the next thing I knew, I was telling this strange, ageing cowboy everything.

Well, not EVERYTHING, obviously, because my DAD was sitting there. Which is apparently some rule of Dr Knutz's, that for the initial consultation of a minor, a parent or guardian has to be present. This wouldn't be the norm if Dr Knutz took me on as a regular patient.

But I told him the important thing – the thing I haven't been able to get out of my head since last Sunday, when I hung up the phone after talking to Michael. The thing that's been keeping me in bed ever since.

And that's that the first time I ever remember Mom and me going to visit her parents back in Versailles, Indiana, Papaw warned me to stay away from the abandoned cistern in the back of the farmhouse, which was covered with an old piece of plywood, and which he was waiting for a backhoe to come and fill in with dirt.

Only I had just read *Alice's Adventures in Wonderland*, and I was obsessed with anything resembling a rabbit hole.

And so of course I moved the plywood off the cistern, and stood there on the edge looking down into the deep dark hole, wondering if it led to Wonderland and if I could really go there.

And of course the dirt around the edge gave way, and I fell down the hole.

Only I didn't end up in Wonderland. Far from it.

I wasn't hurt or anything, and eventually I managed to pull myself out, by grabbing on to roots that were sticking out of the side of the hole. I put the plywood back where it had been, and went back to the house, shaken and smelly and dirty, but no worse for wear. I never told anyone what I'd done, because I knew Papaw would have just gotten mad at me. And fortunately, no one ever found out.

But the thing is, ever since I talked to Michael last Sunday, I've felt as if I was sitting back at the bottom of that hole again. Really. Like I was down there, blinking at the blue sky up above, totally unsure how I'd found myself in this position.

Only this time, there were no roots to pull myself out of the hole. I was stuck down there at the bottom. I could see normal life passing by overhead – people laughing, having fun; the sun beating down; the birds and clouds passing overhead – but I couldn't get back up there to join them. I could just watch, from down at the bottom of that big, black hole.

Anyway, when I was done explaining all this – which was basically when I couldn't talk any more because I was sobbing so hard – my dad started muttering darkly about what he was going to do to Papaw next time he saw him (which seemed to involve a taser).

Dr Knutz, meanwhile, looked up from the piece of paper he'd been writing on the whole time I'd been talking, stared straight into my eyes and said an amazing thing.

He said, 'Sometimes in life, you fall down holes you can't climb out of by yourself. That's what friends and family are for – to help. They can't help, however, unless you let them know you're down there.'

I blinked at him some more. It was really weird but . . . I hadn't thought of that. I know it sounds dumb. But the idea of calling for help had never even occurred to me.

'So now that we do know you're down there,' Dr Knutz drawled on in his Western twang, 'what do you say you let us give you a hand?'

The thing was – I wasn't sure anyone *could*. Help me out of that hole, I mean. I was down there so deep, and I was so tired . . . even if someone threw me a rope, I wasn't certain I'd have the strength to hang on.

'I guess,' I said, sniffling, 'that that would be good. I mean, if it works.'

'It'll work,' Dr Knutz said, matter-of-factly. 'Now, tomorrow morning I want you to pay a visit to your general physician to get a blood work-up, just to make sure there's nothing amiss there. Certain medical conditions can affect mood, so we want to rule those out – along with the meningitis of course. Then you can come see me for your first therapy session after school. Which my office is conveniently located just a few blocks away from.'

I stared at him, my mouth suddenly dry. 'I . . . I really don't think I can go back to school tomorrow.'

'Why not?' Dr Knutz looked surprised.

'I just . . .' I said – my heart had begun to slam into the back of my ribs – 'can't . . . wouldn't it be better if I started back to school on Monday? You know, make a clean start and all that?'

He just looked at me through his silver wire-rimmed glasses. His eyes, I noticed, were blue. The skin around them was crinkly and kind-looking. Just like a cowboy's eyes should look.

'Or maybe,' I said, 'you could, you know. Prescribe me something. Some drugs or something. That might make it easier.'

Ideally some kind of drug that would completely knock me out so I didn't have to think or feel anything until, oh, graduation.

Again, Dr Knutz seemed to know exactly what I meant. And he seemed to find it amusing.

'I'm a psychologist, Mia,' he said with a tiny smile. 'Not a psychiatrist. I can't prescribe drugs. I have a colleague who can, if I feel I have a patient who needs it. But I don't think you do.'

What? He could not be more wrong. I need drugs. A lot of them! Who needs drugs more than me? No one! He was only denying them to me because he hadn't met Grandmere.

The next thing I knew, Dr Knutz was blinking at me, and Dad was wriggling around uncomfortably in his chair. That's when I realized I'd said that last part out loud.

Oops.

'Well,' I said defensively to Dad. 'You know it's true.'

'I know,' Dad said, looking heavenward. 'Believe me.'

'Meeting your grandmother *is* something I look forward to doing someday,' Dr Knutz said. 'She's obviously very important to you, and I'd be interested in seeing the dynamic between you. But again . . . nowhere on this assessment did you indicate that you are feeling suicidal. In fact, when asked if you ever feel like killing yourself, you replied *None of the time*.'

'Well,' I said uncomfortably. 'Only because to kill myself I'd have to get out of bed. And I really don't feel like doing that.'

Dr Knutz smiled and said, 'I don't think drugs are the answer in your particular case.'

'Well, I need *something*,' I said. 'Because otherwise I don't know how I'm going to get through the day. I'm serious. No offence, but you don't know what it's like in high school any more. I'm not kidding, it's scary.'

'You know, Eleanor Roosevelt – a lady few would argue didn't have a good head on her shoulders,' Dr Knutz remarked, 'once said, *Do one thing every day that scares you*.'

I shook my head. 'That makes no sense whatsoever. Why would anybody willingly do things that scare them?'

'Because it's the only way,' Dr Knutz said, 'they'll grow as an individual. Sure, a lot of things can be scary – learning to ride a bike; flying on an airplane for the first time; going back to school after you've broken up with your long-time boyfriend and a picture of you with your best friend's boyfriend has appeared on the cover of a widely distributed newspaper – but if you don't take risks, you'll just stay the same. And is that really how you think you're going to get out of that hole you've fallen into? Don't you think the only way you're going to get out of there is to make a change?'

I took a deep breath. He was right. I knew he was right. It's just . . . it was going to be so *hard*.

Well. Michael *did* say we both had some growing up to do.

Dr Knutz went on, 'And besides, what's the worst thing that can happen? You have a bodyguard. And it's not like you don't have other friends besides Lilly, right? What about this Tina person your mother mentioned?'

I had forgotten about Tina. It's funny how this can happen when you're in a hole. You forget about the people who would do anything – anything in the world, probably – to help you out of it.

'Yes,' I said, feeling, for the first time in a long while, a tiny flicker of hope. 'There's Tina.'

'Well then,' Dr Knutz said. 'There you go. And who knows?' he added, with a grin. 'You might even have fun!'

OK. Now I know his name really *is* appropriate. He's nuttier than I am.

And considering I'm the one who hasn't changed out of her Hello Kitty pyjamas in almost a week, that is saying a lot.

Thursday, September 16, 6 p.m., the Loft

After we left Dr Knutz's office, Dad asked what I thought of him. He said, 'If you don't like him, Mia, we can find someone else. Everyone, including your principal, agrees he's the most highly recommended therapist for adolescents in the city, but—'

'YOU TOLD PRINCIPAL GUPTA?' I practically screamed.

Dad didn't look like he appreciated my screaming very much.

'Mia,' he said, 'you haven't been in school for the past four days. Did you think no one was going to notice?'

'Well, you could have told them I had bronchitis,' I yelled. 'Not that I was depressed!'

'We didn't tell anyone that you're depressed,' Dad said. 'Your principal called to check on why you'd been absent for so long—'

'Great,' I cried, flopping back against the leather seats. 'Now the whole school is going to know!'

'Not unless you tell them,' Dad said. 'Dr Gupta certainly isn't going to say anything to anyone. She's too professional for that. You know that, Mia.'

Much as it pains me to admit it, my dad is right about that. Principal Gupta may be many things – a despotic control freak amongst them – but she would never betray student–principal confidentiality.

Besides, it's not as if at least half the student population of Albert Einstein High School isn't in therapy as well. Still. The last thing I need is *Michael* finding out that I'm so crushed from his rejection of me that I'm seeing a shrink. How humiliating!

'Who else *does* know?' I asked.

'No one knows, Mia,' Dad said. 'You, your mother, your stepfather and Lars here.'

'I won't tell anyone,' Lars said, not looking up from the rousing game of Fantasy Football he was playing on his Treo.

'We're the only ones who know,' Dad went on.

'What about Grandmere?' I asked suspiciously.

'She doesn't know,' Dad said. 'She is, as usual, blissfully ignorant of everything that does not directly involve her.'

'But she's going to figure it out,' I said. 'When I don't show up for princess lessons. She's going to wonder where I am.'

'You let me worry about my mother,' Dad said, looking a little steely-eyed, like Daniel Craig in *Casino Royale*. If James Bond was completely bald. 'You just worry about getting better.'

Which is easy for him to say. He's not the one who's committed to speaking in front of the Opus Dei of women's organizations a week from tomorrow.

Anyway, when I got back to the loft, I found that Mom had used my absence as an opportunity to clean my room and send all my bedding out to the laundry-by-the-pound place. She had also opened all the windows and turned on all the fans and was airing out my room so energetically that Fat Louie wouldn't come out from under the bed for fear of being swept up in the windstorm.

Meanwhile, Mr G had taken away my TV. Which Dad informed me they aren't replacing, because Dr Knutz doesn't believe children should have their own TVs.

So now I know what Dr Knutz and I will be discussing

for a good portion of our appointed hour together tomorrow.

Whatever. I guess I have bigger things to worry about. Like that while I was showering just now, Mom snuck into the bathroom and stole my Hello Kitty pyjamas. And threw them down the incinerator.

'Trust me, Mia,' she said when I confronted her about it. 'It's better this way.'

I guess she's right. Maybe I *was* getting a little too attached to them.

Still. I'll miss them. We went through a lot together, my Hello Kitty pyjamas and me.

Mom, Dad and Mr G are all sitting around the kitchen table right now, having some kind of not-so-secret conference about me. Not-so-secret because I can totally hear. I mean, I might be depressed, but I'm not DEAF.

To distract myself, I went online for the first time in like a million years to see if anyone had emailed me.

It turned out they had. A lot. I had 243 unread messages.

And, OK, most of them were spam. But quite a few were cheerful attempts to make me feel better from Tina. There were some from Ling Su and Shameeka too, and even a couple from Boris (he is such a good boyfriend. He always does exactly what Tina tells him to). There were also quite a few from J.P., mostly funny forwards I guess he thought might cheer me up or something. Not that he knows I'm down. He BETTER not know, anyway.

Then, as I was going through, sending message after message into my Junk mailbox, I saw it.

An email from Michael.

I swear, my heart started beating about a million miles a minute and my palms got instantly soaked. I so didn't want to click on that message. Because what if it was just a reiteration of what he had said to me on Sunday? The thing about how we should just be friends and see other people? I don't want to see that again. I don't want to hear that again. I don't even want to *think* about that again. I've been doing everything I could all week NOT to have to revisit that particular conversation in my mind . . . and now there was a chance of it flashing in front of my eyes?

No way.

But then, just as I was about to hit Delete, I hesitated. Because what if it *wasn't* about that? What if – and OK, I realized this was a big *What if* even as I was thinking it, but whatever – what if it was an email telling me he'd changed his mind and didn't want to break up after all?

What if he'd been as depressed as me this past week (unlikely, since I highly doubt Lilly isn't speaking to him)?

What if, after a week apart, he'd realized how much he misses me, and as much as I was sitting there longing to *be* in his arms, smelling his neck, Michael was longing to *have* me in his arms, smelling his neck?

And before I could change my mind, I clicked Open . . .

Hey, Mia. It's me. Well, obviously. Just checking in to see how you're doing. Lilly tells me you haven't been in school all week . . . hope everything is all right.

I'm settling in here in Tsukuba. This place is a little nutty – they really do eat noodles for breakfast! But fortunately you can still find egg sandwiches most places. The work is what I expected it to be – hard – but I really think I have a solid chance of actually getting this thing off the ground. Although who knows if I'll still feel that optimistic after a few more weeks of this.

Did you see they're supposedly in talks for a Buffy the Vampire Slayer/Angel reunion movie? I thought you'd be excited about that.

Well, I have to go . . . I really hope you're out of school because you've jetted off to somewhere great for princess duty, and not because you've come down with something.

Michael

I sat there for a long time with my finger posed to click Reply. I mean, he'd expressed concern over my health (physical, not mental, but that's OK. I doubt even Michael would have been able to predict I'd hit rock bottom, self-actualization wise, and end up in a cowboy psychologist's office in my Hello Kitty pyjamas and a duvet).

Still, that had to mean something, right? That there's something there? That maybe he still loves me, at least a little? That maybe there's a chance after all that some day, some way, I might be able to smell his neck again, on a semi-regular basis?

But then . . . I don't know. I thought about what he'd said on the phone. About just wanting to be friends. That's all, I realized, this email was. A friendly note to show he had no hard feelings over the J.P. thing.

HOW COULD HE HAVE NO HARD FEELINGS OVER THAT? HADN'T HE CARED ABOUT ME *AT ALL*?????

Or had I, in the complete psychotic break I had last week over the Judith Gershner thing, managed to destroy any iota of romantic feeling he ever had for me?

Which is when I moved my mouse from the Reply button to Delete. And pressed.

And just like that, his email was gone.

And no way was I writing back to him.

Michael may be over me. But I'm not over him. Not yet, anyway.

And I can't pretend like I am. And I'm not going to do something stupid and undignified like hit Reply and ask him to take me back.

But the only way I know how not to do that is just not to say anything to him at all.

After I deleted Michael's email, I checked ihatemia-thermopolis.com. There were no new updates, thank God.

Well, why would there be? I haven't been out of the house all week. Whoever is running the site doesn't have any new material.

Now Mom's calling me. She and Dad and Mr G have ordered pizza from Tre Giovanni's. We're all going to sit down to dinner like a normal family. Just me, my mom, her husband, their kid, and my dad, the Prince of Genovia.

Oh, yeah. We're a normal family, all right.

No wonder I'm in therapy.

Friday, September 17, French

Oh my God. It is so . . . surreal, being here.

I think Dr K was wrong, and I do need drugs. Because I just don't see how else I'm going to cope. I know he said it's good to do one thing every day that scares you – thanks for that, by the way, Eleanor Roosevelt. Thanks a lot – but this is like NINE MILLION THINGS all at once.

And, yeah, OK, I don't know why SCHOOL should be so scary. I was never scared of school before. At least, not this much.

But there's so much more to it than just school. There's having to TALK to people. There's having to act NORMAL. When I know I'm NOT normal.

And, OK, the truth is I've never been normal. But I am more NOT normal than ever. I have lost my support system – the ONE thing I have been able to count on for almost the past two years now to keep me sane in this sea of complete insanity – Michael.

And now, just like that, he's gone – completely ripped from my life – and I'm just supposed to go on like nothing's happened? Yeah. Right.

And I have to be here, in this – let's face it – nut house, with all these people who are WAY CRAZIER THAN I AM (they just won't admit there's anything wrong with them. Unlike me) with absolutely no one to look forward to going home to and saying, 'Oh my God, you would not believe what so-and-so did today.'

Seriously, that is just cruel.

But I guess it's what I deserve. I mean, it isn't as if I didn't bring all this upon myself with my own stupidity.

At least I haven't been forced to suffer the onslaught

of a full day of this place. I got to spend my morning waiting around Dr Fung's office to get my blood drawn. And since I'd had to fast since midnight the night before, in order for my blood work not to get messed up, I was practically STARVING. I mean, it was bad enough I actually had to get out of bed, shower and get dressed.

But I didn't even get breakfast!

Worse, even though my belly was totally empty, I couldn't . . . well, for some reason my uniform skirt wouldn't close. I mean, it would zip – mostly – but I couldn't get the button to go through the slot, because there was all this SKIN in the way. I finally had to use a safety pin in the end to keep my skirt on.

At first I thought my skirt must have shrunk at the cleaners and I was kind of mad about it.

But my bra didn't fit either! I mean, I realize it's been a while since I put on any underwear, since I was in my Hello Kitty pyjamas for most of the week.

And I will admit I noticed things have been getting a little snug all over lately. And I've been wearing only my jeans with stretch in them. And having to use the last hooks on all my bras.

And even then they leave marks on me.

But when I put on my favourite bra this morning, for the first time in my life, I actually had CLEAVAGE, because it was squeezing my boobs so tight.

That's right. I actually *have* boobs to be squeezed. I don't know where they came from, but I looked down and there they were. Hello! Boobs!

So then I thought maybe the laundry-by-the-pound place had shrunk my bra too. So I tried a different one. Same thing. Then another. SAME THING. I couldn't understand it.

But when I got to the SoHo Medical Clinic and they FINALLY called my name, I went in and they weighed me, and I found out what was going on. I was SHOCKED to find that I weigh almost SIX Fat Louies!

That is nearly one more Fat Louie than I weighed last time I stepped on a scale! Which I'll admit was a while ago, but still!

And, OK, maybe I've been hitting the meat kind of hard this past week or so. Well, not just the meat either, but the pizza, the Girl Scout Cookies, the peanut butter, the cold sesame noodles, the Honey Nut Cheerios, the microwave popcorn (with melted butter), the Oreos, the Häagen-Dazs and the fried samosas from Baluchi's . . .

But to have gained almost a whole CAT?

Wow. That is all I have to say. Just . . . wow.

Of course, there was a rational explanation, beyond the meat. Dr Fung went, 'You're still well within the body-mass-index range for your height, Princess. It's actually quite normal to have these sorts of growth spurts at your age. Some women have them even into their twenties.'

Because I haven't just grown out. I've grown up – I'm five feet ten inches now. I grew another whole INCH since the last time I was at the doctor's office!

If I keep going like this, I'll be six feet tall by the time I'm eighteen.

On the bright side of gaining a whole Fat Louie? I guess I'm not flat-chested any more.

On the not-so-bright side? I'm going to have to talk to Mom about getting new bras. And panties. And jeans. And pyjamas. And sweats. And a new school uniform.

And new ballgowns.

Oh, God.

But whatever. Like I don't have way bigger things to worry about (ha) than the size of my chest (gargantuan) and the fact that my skirt is being held together by pieces of metal and all my jeans are too short. I mean, there's the fact that in half an hour I'm going to have to go down to the cafeteria.

And see Lilly.

Who will no doubt take her tray and go sit elsewhere when she sees me.

Which . . . well, whatever. I know Tina will still want to sit with me. That is the only thing, in fact, that is keeping me from turning to Lars and going, 'We're leaving,' and marching straight out of this loony bin.

In fact it's a good thing Dr Knutz mentioned Tina yesterday, because every time I start to feel too much like I am slipping back down this hole I'm trying to crawl out of, I think of her, and it's like she's a root or something I can grab hold of to keep from sliding further into the black abyss of despair.

I wonder how Tina would feel if she found out I think of her as a root?

Of course, I have way worse things to worry about than who I'm going to sit with at lunch: the fact that I'm in therapy and I don't want anyone to know; the fact that in a week's time I'm allegedly going to have to give an address to a couple of thousand of New York City's most influential businesswomen; the fact that the love of my life just wants to be friends (and see other people) and that I no longer have him to be my loving support system and so have been cast adrift to swim the social seas of adolescence alone; the fact that the meat industry pumps so many hormones into their products that, just by consuming a few dozen ham sandwiches and servings of kung pao chicken over the past week, I have finally managed to grow breasts virtually overnight; ihatemiathermopolis.com; the fact that both the polar ice caps are melting due to anthropogenic global warming and the polar bears are all drowning.

But I'm trying to take all my worries one at a time. Baby steps, like Rocky took when he was first starting to walk. Baby steps. First I need to get through lunch. Then I'll worry about the polar ice caps.

Four more hours until I can get out of here.

Friday, September 17, Gifted and Talented

Great. So now I have another worry to add to the list:

Apparently, the entire school thinks J.P. and I are going out.

This is what happens when you are gone for almost a week having a nervous breakdown and aren't around to defend yourself.

Well, I guess it's also what happens when you have your picture splattered all over the place coming out of a theatre arm in arm with a guy. But he was only helping me down the steps! Because I was in heels! And the steps were carpeted and there were no handrails!

Jeez!

And OK, based on the photographic evidence, I could see why middle America – and the rest of the world, I guess – would think J.P. and I are going out.

Still! You'd think my own FRIENDS would know better!

But apparently not. And the line in the sand has already been drawn:

Lilly now sits at Kenny Showalter's lunch table.

I guess their mutual appreciation for his Muay Thai fighting friends has drawn them together or something.

Perin and Ling Su sit with them, although Ling Su told me, over at the taco bar, that she'd rather sit with me.

'But Lilly appointed me secretary,' she explained, sounding genuinely dismayed about it. 'Which is better than treasurer, I guess –' This is definitely true, given what happened when Ling Su was treasurer last year – 'which is what Lilly appointed Kenny. But it means I have to sit with her and Perin, who's vice-president, so we can talk about Lilly's new initiatives, like this whole renting-the-roof-for-cellphone-towers-in-exchange-for-free-laptops-for-scholarship-students thing, and how we're going to guarantee more AEHS students get into the Ivy League school of their choice, and that kind of thing.'

'It's OK, Ling Su,' I said to her as I sprinkled cheddar cheese over my spicy beef tostada. 'Really. I understand.'

'Good. And just for the record,' she added, 'I think you and J.P. make an awesome couple. He's so hot.'

'We're not going out,' I said, totally confused.

'Right,' Ling Su said knowingly, and winked at me. Like she thought I was just saying that, in some kind of misguided attempt to stay on Lilly's good side! Which would have been so totally futile, if that's why I'd said it. But that *isn't* why I said it at all! I said it because it was true!

But Ling Su's not the only one who thinks J.P. and I are an item. When I went to return my lunch tray, one of the cafeteria workers smiled at me and said, 'Maybe you can get him to give our corn a try.'

At first I couldn't figure out what she was talking about. Then, when I did, I totally started blushing. J.P.'s notorious hatred for corn! And she thought *I* could cure him of it? Oh God!

At least J.P. doesn't appear to realize what's going on. Or, if he does know, he isn't letting on. He seemed *surprised* to see me show up at lunch for the first time all week, but he didn't make a big deal out of it (thank God) the way Tina did, by squealing and hugging me and telling me how much she'd missed me.

Which was very nice, but sort of embarrassing, since

it drew even more attention to the fact that I've been gone so long, and I'm totally tired of going, 'Bronchitis,' when people ask me where I was all week. Because I can't exactly go, 'In my Hello Kitty pyjamas in bed, refusing to get up after my boyfriend dumped me.'

The only thing J.P. did that was at all out of the ordinary was smile at me when there was nothing to smile about – Boris was actually going on about his hatred for emo, specifically My Chemical Romance, as he is wont to do. I was taking a big bite of my taco – it's amazing how, even though I'm totally depressed, I'm still eating like a horse. But whatever, I was starving. All I'd had to eat all day was a power bar I picked up at Ho's Deli after my doctor's appointment, on my way into school – and noticed J.P.'s smile (which, like Ling Su said, really is pretty hot) and went, 'What?' with my mouth all full of chopped beef, cheddar cheese, salsa, sour cream, jalapeños and shredded lettuce.

'Nothing,' J.P. said, still smiling. 'I'm just glad you're back. Don't stay away so long again, OK?'

Which was nice of him. Especially considering the fact that he MUST know people are saying we're an item.

Which would at least partially explain why Lilly is sticking so assiduously to her side of the G and T room. She won't look at me – won't speak to me – won't let on that I even exist. To her, I'm apparently Hester Prynne from *The Scarlet Letter*.

Only the book, not the movie version, in which Hester Prynne was played by Demi Moore and was semi-cool and blew stuff up. Oh, wait . . . that was *G.I. Jane*.

I wish I could just go up to Lilly and be like, 'Look.

I'm SORRY. I'm sorry I was such an ass to your brother, and I'm sorry if I did anything to hurt you. But don't you think I've been punished enough? I can barely BREATHE now because there's NO POINT in breathing if I know that at the end of the day I can't smell your brother's neck. All I can think about is how I will never, ever again hear the sound of his sarcastic laughter as we watch *South Park* together. Can you not see that it took every ounce of courage and strength I possess just to come here today? That I'm in THERAPY? That I spend every single second of the day wishing I was DEAD? So do you think you could drop the cold shoulder thing and cut me some slack? Because I really do value and miss your friendship. And by the way, do you really think hooking up with random Muay Thai fighters is the most mature way to respond to your heartache? Are you supposed to be Lana Weinberger or somebody?'

Only I can't. Because I don't think I could bear to see that dead-eyed thing she does whenever she looks at me now.

Because I know that's exactly how she'll respond.

Friday, September 17, PE

I'm standing here, shaking.

Standing and not sitting, because I'm in one of the ball fields on the Great Lawn in Central Park. I guess I'm playing left outfield or something, but it's hard to tell with all the yelling. *Get the ball! Get the ball!*

As if. *You* get the ball, loser. Can't you see I'm busy writing in my journal?

I totally should have made Dr Fung give me a note to get me out of PE. WHAT WAS I THINKING?

Because it's not just this *Get the ball* thing. I had to DISROBE in front of everybody. Which meant I had to lift up my sweater, and everyone saw the SAFETY PIN holding my skirt together.

I went, 'Ha ha, lost a button.'

But that didn't explain why, when I put on my gym shorts, they were SKIN TIGHT and gave me total cameltoe. Thank God my gym T was always a little too big to begin with. Now it fits just right.

As if all that wasn't bad enough, somehow LANA WEINBERGER ended up being in the locker room when I was changing.

I don't know what she was doing there since she doesn't even have PE this period. I guess she didn't like the way her hair was curling or something, because she was giving herself another blow-dry. Eva Braun, aka Trisha Hayes, was standing right next to her, filing her nails.

And of course, even though I ducked my head instinctively as soon as I saw them, hoping they wouldn't notice me, it was too late. Lana must have spied my reflection in the mirror she was gazing into or something, because next thing I know, she'd switched the hairdryer off, and was going, 'Oh, there you are. Where have *you* been all week?'

LIKE SHE'D BEEN LOOKING FOR ME!

See, this is EXACTLY why I didn't want to go back to school. I can't deal with stuff like this on TOP of all the other stuff that's going on. Seriously, my head is going to explode.

'Um,' I said. 'Bronchitis.'

'Oh,' Lana said. 'Well, about that letter you got from my mother –'

I closed my eyes. I actually CLOSED MY EYES because I knew what was coming next – or thought I did anyway – and I didn't think I was emotionally capable of dealing with it.

'Yes,' I said. And inside, I was thinking, *Just say it. Whatever mean, bitter, humiliating thing you're going to say, just say it, so I can get out of here. Please. I don't know how much more of this I can take.*

'Thanks for saying yes,' was the totally astonishing thing Lana said instead. 'Because Angelina Jolie was supposed to do it, but she totally dropped out to play Mother Teresa in some new movie instead. Mom was driving me crazy, she was so frantic to find a replacement. So I suggested you. You gave that speech last year, you know, when we were both running for student council president. And it was kind of good. So I figured you'd be a decent sub for Angelina. So. Thanks.'

I'm not positive. We'll have to check with seismologists worldwide. But I truly think at that moment, hell actually froze over.

Because Lana Weinberger said something nice to me.

That, of course, isn't the part that makes me wish I'd gotten a note from Dr Fung excusing me from PE today, however.

This next part is.

I was so astonished that Lana Weinberger was actually acting like a human being that I couldn't reply right away. I just stood there staring at her. Which unfortunately gave Trisha Hayes a chance to notice the safety pin holding my skirt closed.

And she's way too savvy to believe the lost-button excuse.

'Dude,' Trisha said. 'You like totally need a new skirt.' Then her gaze flicked up towards my chest. 'And a bigger bra.'

I could feel myself turning bright, bright red. It's a good thing I have an appointment with a therapist after school today. Because we're going to have SO much to talk about.

'I know,' I said. 'I, um, need to go shopping.'

Which is when the next totally astounding thing happened. Lana turned back towards her reflection and, running her fingers through her now stick-straight hair, said, 'We're going to the lingerie trunk show at Bendel's tomorrow. Wanna come with?'

'Dude, are you—' *insane*, was clearly what Trisha was going to ask.

But I saw Lana cut her a warning glance in the mirror, and just like Admiral Piett when he realized he'd let the Millennium Falcon get away right in front of Darth Vader, Trisha shut her mouth . . . though she looked scared.

I just stood there, not sure if any of this was really happening, or if it was a symptom of my depression.

Maybe I have some form of depression where you hallucinate invitations to lingerie trunk shows at Bendel's from cheerleaders who've always hated you. You never know.

When I didn't reply right away, Lana turned around to face me. For once, she didn't look snobby. She just looked . . . normal.

'Look,' she said. 'I know you and I haven't always gotten along, Mia. That thing with Josh . . . well, whatever. He was such a jerk sometimes. Plus, some of your friends are really . . . I mean, that Lilly girl—'

'Say no more,' I said, raising a hand. I wasn't just saying it either. Because I really meant it. I really didn't want Lana to say anything more about Lilly. Who, it's true, has been treating me like dirt lately.

But maybe I deserve to be treated like dirt.

'Yeah, well,' Lana went on. 'I saw you weren't sitting with her at lunch today.'

'We're having,' I said stiffly, 'a time out.'

'Well, whatever,' Lana said. 'You're really bailing my mom out of a jam. And if you're going to be a Domina Rei some day, like I will – with any luck – then I think we ought to let bygones be bygones. I mean, we're hopefully a little more mature than we used to be, and can be grown up about this. Don't you think?'

I was so shocked I just nodded.

Instead of pointing out that it isn't so much that Lana and I haven't gotten along, as that she's been totally mean to some of my friends.

Instead of going, 'For your information, I wouldn't be a Domina Rei if you paid me.'

Instead of doing any of those things, I just stood there and nodded.

Because I couldn't think of anything else to do. That's how completely astonished I was by what was going on.

Or how crazy depressed I am about everything.

'Cool,' Lana said. 'So tomorrow morning, ten o'clock, at Bendel's. We'll do lunch somewhere after. If you want. Come on, Trish. We gotta get to class.'

And, just like that, the two of them walked out . . .

. . . at almost the exact same time that Mrs Potts came in and blew her whistle and told us to get in line to go to the park.

I did what I was told without even thinking about it. That's how much of a daze I was in from what had just happened. A part of me was going, *It's a trick. It has to be. I'm going to get to Bendel's, and instead of Lana, David Hasselhoff is going to be there, along with all these paparazzi, who'll take pictures of me and The Hoff together, and the headline in all the Sunday papers will be,* Meet the New Future Royal Consort of Genovia . . . David Hasselhoff!

But the rational part of me – I guess, even as sunk in depression as I am, there's still a rational side of me – was telling me that *OBVIOUSLY Lana was being sincere. The thing she said about Josh – I mean, basically, what happened between you and Josh and Lana is no different than what's happening now between you and J.P. and Lilly. Even though you and J.P. are just friends, Lilly still THINKS you stole him, same as Lana thought about Josh. The only difference really was that you were actually crushing on Josh. No wonder Lana was mad. No wonder LILLY is mad. God, Mia. You do suck.*

So maybe it's not a trick after all. Maybe Lana really does want to hang out with me.

The question is . . . do I really want to hang out with her?

Oh, crud. Here comes Mrs Potts. She doesn't look too happy about the fact that I've brought my journal out to left field with me to write all this.

But is it my fault no one will throw the ball to me?

Friday, September 17, Chemistry

Oh, God.

As far as I can tell, utter bedlam has overtaken this class since I've been gone. We've broken off into individual group experiments of our choice. The one Kenny and J.P. have chosen in my absence appears to be something called nitro starch synthesis, which, they inform me, is actually 'a mixture of several nitrate esters of starch with the formula $[C_6H_7(OH)_x(ONO_2)_y]_n$ where $x+y3$ and n is any whole number from one on up'.

I have no idea what any of that means. I've just put on my goggles and my lab coat, and am sitting here holding stuff out to them when they ask for it.

When I can actually identify what it is that they want, anyway.

I think I'm still in shock from the whole Lana incident. I have to figure out how I'm going to get out of going to the lingerie trunk show at Bendel's with Lana Weinberger tomorrow.

True, I totally do need new bras. But how can I hang out with *Lana*? I mean, even if she *did* apologize. She's still . . . Lana. What do we have in common? She likes partying. I like lying in my bed in my Hello Kitty flannel pyjamas watching *Why I Wore Lipstick to My Mastectomy*.

Which reminds me. I can't go shopping at Bendel's tomorrow. There's no school tomorrow, which means I can spend the whole day in bed. YES!!! I love my bed. It's safe in there. No one can get me there.

Except that Mr G took my TV away.

Oh, well. I can always read *Jane Eyre* again. I mean, there's that whole part in it where Jane and Mr

Rochester get separated because of the whole Bertha thing, and then she hears his disembodied voice floating over the moor . . . Maybe I'll hear Michael's disembodied voice floating over the Hudson, and know that deep down he still loves me and wants me back, and then I can fly to Japan and –

> *Mia! What are you doing tomorrow night? If I got tickets to something, would you come with me? Anything you want to see, you name it. – J.P.*

Oh, God. What can I say? I just want to stay in bed. Forever.

> That's sweet, J.P., but I'm still not quite over my bronchitis. I think I'm going to lay low. Thanks for thinking of me though! – M

> *That's cool! If you want, I could come over. We could watch some movies . . .*

Oh, wow. J.P. is really taking this break-up with Lilly hard. Even though he, of course, is the one who initiated it. Still, he can't even stand the thought of being alone on a Saturday night.

> I'd love to, but the truth is, my TV is on the fritz.

Which isn't the truth at all. But is about as much of the truth as J.P. is ever going to get.

> *Mia, is this about the newspaper thing? Everybody thinking we're going out? Are the paparazzi staking*

out your place or something? You don't want to be caught being seen with me, a mere commoner, again?

Oh, God.

NO! Of course not! I'm just really beat, J.P. It's been a long week.

OK. I can take a hint. There's someone else, isn't there? It's Kenny, right? You two are engaged? When's the wedding? Where are you registered? Sharper Image, right? You guys want an iJoy 550 robotic massage chair, don't you?

I couldn't help bursting out laughing at that. Which of course made Mr Hipskin look over at our table and go, 'Is there a problem, people?'

'No,' Kenny said, then glared at us.

'Could you two,' Kenny hissed, 'quit passing notes and *help*?'

'Absolutely,' J.P. said. 'What do you want us to do?'

'Well, for starters,' Kenny said. 'You could pass me the starch.'

Which reminded me:

'So, Kenny,' I said, just as Kenny was sprinkling some white stuff into a jar of other white stuff, 'what's this I hear about Lilly hooking up with some Muay Thai fighter friend of yours at her party Saturday night?'

Kenny nearly dropped the white stuff. Then he gave me a very irritated look.

'Mia,' he said 'with all due respect. I am in the

middle of a hazardous procedure involving the use of highly corrosive acids. Please can we talk about Lilly some other time?'

God! What a baby.

Friday, September 17, Limo on the way home from Dr Knutz's office

Seriously, I don't know which is worse: princess lessons or therapy. I mean, they are both equally horrible, in their own way.

But at least with princess lessons, I get the POINT. I'm being prepared to one day rule a country. With therapy, it's like . . . I don't even KNOW what the point is. Because if it's supposed to be making me feel better, it's NOT.

And there's HOMEWORK. I mean, like I don't have ENOUGH to do with a week of school to make up. I have to do homework on my PSYCHE too?

I seriously don't know what we're paying Dr Knutz for, when he's making ME do all the work.

Like, today's session started off with Dr Knutz asking me how school went. We were alone in his office this time – Dad wasn't there, because this was a real session and not a consultation. Everything was exactly the same as last time . . . crazy cowboy decor, wire-rimmed glasses, white hair and all.

The only difference really was that I was in my too-small school uniform instead of my Hello Kitty pyjamas. Which I told him my mom had put down the incinerator. The same night my stepfather took away my TV.

To which Dr Knutz replied, 'Good. Now. What happened in school today?'

So then I told him – ONCE AGAIN – that I don't even get why I have to GO to school, since I already have complete job assurance after graduation ANY-WAY, and I hate it, so why can't I just stay home?

Then Dr Knutz asked me why I hate school so much, and so – just to illustrate my point – I told him about Lana.

But he totally didn't get it. He was like, 'But isn't that a good thing? A girl with whom you haven't gotten along in the past made a friendly overture towards you. She is willing to move on from your past differences. Isn't that what you'd like your friend Lilly to do?'

'Yeah,' I said, amazed he couldn't understand something so obvious. 'But I LIKE Lilly. Lana's been nothing but mean to me.'

'And Lilly's been kind lately?'

'Well, not LATELY. But she thinks I stole her boyfriend . . .' My voice trailed off as I remembered that I'd once stolen Lana's boyfriend too. 'OK,' I said. 'I get your point. But . . . should I really go *shopping* with Lana Weinberger tomorrow?'

'Do YOU think you should go shopping with Lana tomorrow?' Dr Knutz wanted to know.

Seriously. This is what we're paying some ungodly amount of money for.

'I don't know!' I cried. 'I'm asking you!'

'But you know yourself better than I do.'

'How can you even say that?' I practically yelled. '*Everyone* knows me better than I do! Haven't you see the movies of my life? Because if not, you're the only one in the world who hasn't!'

'I might,' Dr Knutz admitted, 'have ordered them from Netflix. But they haven't come yet. I only met you yesterday, remember. And I'm more of a Western fan myself.'

I rolled my eyes at all the mustang portraits. 'Gee,' I said, 'I couldn't tell.'

'So,' Dr Knutz said. 'What else?'

I blinked at him. 'What do you mean, what else? Except for the fact that, I reiterate, my STEPDAD TOOK AWAY MY TV!!!'

'Do you know what the one thing every student who has ever been admitted to West Point has in common?'

Hello. Random. 'No. But I guess you're gonna tell me.'

'None of them had a television in their room.'

'BUT I DON'T WANT TO GO TO WEST POINT,' I yelled.

Dr Knutz, however, doesn't respond to yelling. He just went, 'What else about your school do you hate?'

Where to begin? 'Well, how about the fact that everybody thinks I'm dating a guy I'm not?' I asked. 'Just because it said so in the *New York Post*? And the fact that the guy I *do* like – whom I, in fact, love – is sending me emails asking how I am, like nothing happened between us, and that he didn't yank my heart out of my chest and kick it across the room, like we're *friends* or something?'

Dr Knutz looked confused. 'But didn't you agree with Michael that the two of you *should* just be friends?'

'Yes,' I said frustratedly. 'But I didn't mean it!'

'I see. Well, how did you respond to his email?'

'I didn't,' I said, suddenly feeling a bit ashamed. 'I deleted it.'

'Why did you do that?' Dr Knutz wanted to know.

'I don't know,' I said. 'I just . . . I didn't trust myself not to beg him to take me back. And I don't want to be that girl.'

'That's a valid reason for deleting his email,' Dr Knutz said. And for some reason – even though he's a COWBOY THERAPIST – I felt pleased by this. 'Now. Why don't you want to go shopping with your friend?'

I stopped feeling so pleased. Could he not PAY ATTENTION TO THE SIMPLEST DETAIL?

'I told you. She's not my friend. She's my enemy. If you had seen the movies—'

'I'll watch them this weekend,' he said.

'All right. But . . . the thing is . . . her mom asked me to speak at this event. And Grandmere says it's a big honour. And she's super-excited about it. And it turns out Lara's mom asked me because Lana recommended me. Which was . . . decent of her.'

'So that,' Dr Knutz said, 'is why you didn't turn down her invitation to go shopping right away?'

'Well, that, and . . . I need new clothes. And Lana knows a lot about shopping. And if I'm supposed to do one thing every day that scares me – well, the idea of shopping with Lana Weinberger DEFINITELY scares me.'

'Then I think you have your answer,' Dr K said.

'But I'd much rather spend my whole day in bed,' I said quickly. 'Reading,' I added. 'OR WATCHING TV.'

'Back on the ranch,' Dr Knutz said in his cowboy drawl, 'we've got a mare named Dusty.'

I think my mouth actually fell open. Dusty? After all that, he was actually telling me a story about a mare named *Dusty*? What kind of weird psychological technique *was* this?

'Whenever it's a hot summer day and Dusty passes a certain pretty little pond on my property,' Dr Knutz went on, 'she wades off into the middle of it. It doesn't matter if she's saddled up and has a rider on her. Dusty doesn't care. She's got to get into that water. Want to know why?'

I was so shocked by the fact that a trained psychologist would tell me a story about a HORSE in a professional setting that I just nodded dumbly.

'Because,' Dr Knutz said. 'She's hot. And she wants to cool off. She'd rather spend the day in that pond than carry somebody around on her back. But we don't always get to do what we want to do. Because it's not necessarily healthy or practical. Besides, saddles are ruined when they get wet.'

I stared at him.

And this guy was supposed to be the nation's preeminent adolescent and child psychologist?

'I want to go back to something you said yesterday,' Dr Knutz said without waiting for me to respond to the Dusty story. Thank God. 'You said, and I quote –' And he DID quote. He actually read from his notes – '*Maybe it's a little more complicated than a normal teenagers' break-up, because I'm a princess and Michael is a genius, and he thinks he has to go off to Japan to build a robotic surgical arm in order to prove to my family that he's worthy of me, when the truth is, I'm not worthy of him, and I suppose because deep down inside I know that, I completely sabotaged our relationship.*'

He looked up from his notes. 'What did you mean by that?'

'I meant –' This was all going too fast for me. I'd barely gotten over being shocked by the Dusty story, and still hadn't been able to figure out what it had to do with me going bra shopping with Lana Weinberger tomorrow – 'that I guess I figured he was going to dump me for a smarter, more accomplished girl anyway. So I beat him to the punch by dumping him first. Even though I regretted it later. The whole Judith Gershner thing . . . I mean, the reason it upset me so much is because I know deep down inside that that's who he should really be with. Someone who can clone fruit flies. Not someone like . . . like m-me, who's j-just a p-princess.'

And before I knew it, I was crying again. Man! What was it about this guy's office that made me weep like a baby?

Dr Knutz passed me the tissues. Not in an unkindly way either.

'Did he ever do or say anything to make you think this?' he wanted to know.

'N-no,' I sobbed.

'Then why do you think you feel that way?'

'B-because it's true! I mean, being a princess is no big accomplishment! I was just BORN this way! I didn't EARN it, the way Michael is going to earn fame and fortune from his robotic surgical arm. I mean, anyone can be BORN!'

'I think,' Dr Knutz said a little drily, 'you're being a bit hard on yourself. You're only sixteen. Very few sixteen-year-olds actually—'

'JUDITH GERSHNER HAD ALREADY CLONED HER FIRST FRUIT FLY BY THE TIME SHE WAS SIXTEEN!' I shouted.

Then I felt ashamed of myself. I mean, for shouting. But I couldn't help it.

'And look at Lilly,' I went on. 'She's sixteen, and she has her own TV show. And sure, it's on public access, but whatever, it's been optioned. And she has thousands of loyal viewers. And she made that show, all by herself.

No one even helped her. Well, except for me and Shameeka and Ling Su and Tina. But we just helped with the camera work really. So saying I'm only sixteen – that doesn't mean anything. There are lots of sixteen-year-olds who have accomplished loads more than me. I can't even get published in *Sixteen* magazine.'

'Supposing I take your word for it,' Dr Knutz said. 'If you really feel that way – that you aren't worthy of Michael – hadn't you better do something about it?'

Truly. He said that. He didn't say, *Gosh, Mia, how can you say you're not worthy of Michael? Of course you're worthy! You're a fabulous human being, so giving and full of life*.

Which is basically what everyone else has been saying to me whenever I have brought up this subject.

No, he was like, *Yeah, you're right. You do kind of suck. Now what are you going to do about it?*

I was so shocked I stopped crying and just sat there staring at him with my mouth hanging open.

'Aren't you . . . aren't you supposed to say that I'm great just the way I am?' I demanded.

He shrugged. 'What would be the point? You wouldn't believe it anyway.'

'Well, aren't you *at least* supposed to say I should want to improve my worth for *myself*? As opposed to for some *boy*?'

'I assumed that was a given,' Dr K said.

'Well,' I said. I was still kind of trying to get over my shock. 'I mean, it's true. I *do* have to do something to prove I'm more than just a princess. Only . . . what? What can I do?'

Dr Knutz shrugged. 'How should I know? I still have to watch the movies of your life in order to get to know you as well as you claim they'll make me. But I'll tell you one thing I *do* know: You're not going to find out by lying around in bed, not going to school . . . or by continuing to hold grudges against people simply because they've said some unpleasant things to you in the past.'

Unpleasant? Wait till he gets a load of ihatemiathermopolis.com. Not that I've given him the URL. Or told him that Lana's behind it.

But still. He doesn't know the meaning of unpleasant.

So. My assignment?

1. Go shopping with Lana.

2. Figure out what I was put on this planet for (besides being a princess).

3. Come back and see Dr Knutz next Friday after school.

I think I can handle the last one. The first two, though? Might actually kill me.

Friday, September 17, 7 p.m., the Loft

Inbox: 0

Not that I actually expected to hear from either
Michael OR Lilly. Especially not after I deleted
Michael's email without even replying to it, and the way
Lilly ignored me in G and T.

Still. I had kind of hoped . . . I mean, this is the
longest she's not spoken to me. Ever.

I just can't believe it's basically over between us.

And because of a BOY.

Tina just IM'd me though. At least I still have Tina.

```
Iluvromance: Mia! How ARE you? I barely got to
             talk to you at school today. Are
             you feeling better?
>
FtLouie:     Yes, thanks!
```

Whatever. I lie all the time anyway.

```
Iluvromance: I'm so glad! You looked so sad at
             school.
>
FtLouie:     Well. Yeah. I guess that's kind
             of to be expected, considering
             the fact I've lost the love of my
             life and all.
>
Iluvromance: I know. I'm so, so sorry. Hey, I
             know what might cheer you up!
             Some retail therapy! I mean, you
```

did grow an inch and gained a
whole size! You need new
clothes! Do you want to go
shopping tomorrow? My mom'll
take us. You know how she loves
to shop!!!

Which is so totally what I get for ever having agreed to
go shopping with Lana. Because Tina's mom is practically a shopping GENIUS, being a former model and
all. *And* she knows all the designers.

FtLouie: Oh, I'd love to! But I have to
              do something with my grand-
              mother.

The lies just keep mounting and mounting. But whatever. I can't tell TINA I'm doing something with LANA
WEINBERGER. She'd never understand it. Even if I
explained about the Do-One-Thing-Every-Day-That-
Scares-You thing. And the thing about the Domina Reis.

Iluvromance: Oh. OK. Well, what are you doing
             tomorrow night then? Want to
             come over? My parents are going
             out and I have to babysit, but we
             can watch some DVDs or some-
             thing.

For some reason – well, OK, I guess because I'm
depressed – this invitation almost made me cry. I mean,
Tina is just so sweet.

Also, it sounded like something I could handle, emo-

106

tionally. As opposed to going out with the guy I'd recently been accused of being in love with by the media. When the truth is, I've only ever loved one guy, and he is currently in Japan, sending me random emails about how hard it is to find egg sandwiches there.

Yeah. Nice.

```
FtLouie:      I can't think of anything I'd
              rather do.
```

Except lie in my own bed and watch TV.

But my TV got taken away. So I can't even do that.

```
Iluvromance: Yay! I was thinking we should
             re-examine the Drew Barrymore
             oeuvre. Her less recent works,
             like Ever After and The Wedding
             Singer.
>
FtLouie:     That sounds PERFECT. I'll bring
             the popcorn.
```

I really don't feel guilty about not telling Tina about Michael's email . . . or about the fact that I'm in therapy. Because I'm just not ready to talk about those things with anybody yet.

Maybe some day I will be.

But first? I'm going to take a really long nap.

Because I'm exhausted.

Saturday, September 18, 10 a.m., Bendel's Luxury Department Store

What am I doing here?

I don't belong in a store like this. Stores like this are for FANCY people.

And OK, I'm a princess. Which is admittedly pretty fancy.

But I am currently wearing a pair of my MOM'S jeans, because none of my own fits me.

People who are wearing MOM jeans do not belong in stores like these, which are all golden and sparkly and filled with attractive model-types carrying bottles of perfume, who come up to you and go, 'Trish McEvoy?'

And when you go, 'No, my name is Mia –' they spritz you with something that smells like Febreze, only fruitier.

I'm not kidding. This is not the Gap. It's more the kind of store Grandmere hangs out in. Only more crowded. Because usually when Grandmere shops, she calls ahead and has the store opened up for her after hours so she can shop without having to rub elbows with any commoners.

Mom just about had a coronary when I told her where I was going this morning – and why I needed to borrow her jeans.

'You're going shopping with WHOM????'

'I don't want to talk about it,' I said. 'It's something I have to do. For therapy.'

'Your therapist is making you go shopping with *Lana Weinberger?*' Mom exchanged glances with Mr G, who was refilling Rocky's cereal bowl with Cheerios, and who had gotten so distracted by our conversation that he'd accidentally caused Cheerios to overflow the bowl and fall all the way down the sides of Rocky's booster chair. Which delighted Rocky no end. 'This is supposed to help ALLEVIATE your depression?'

'It's a long story,' I said to her. 'I'm supposed to do something every day that scares me.'

'Well,' Mom said, handing over her Levi's. 'Shopping with Lana Weinberger would scare me.'

Mom's right. What am I doing here? Why did I listen to Dr K anyway? What does HE know about the long, torrid history between Lana and me? Nothing! He's never even seen the movies of my life! He doesn't know all the heinous things she's done to me and my friends in the past! He has no way of knowing that this whole shopping thing is probably a trick! That David Hasselhoff is the only one who is going to show up! That making me come here and stand among the perfume spritzers waiting for The Hoff is Lana's idea of a grand, final joke –

Oh. Here she comes.

More later.

Saturday, September 18, 3 p.m., Bathroom at Nobu Fifty Seven

For reasons that are completely beyond me, Lana Weinberger and her clone, Trisha Hayes, are actually being nice to me.

Actually the reasons aren't completely beyond me. Lana already told me why she's being so nice to me: 'Because I'm finally over the Josh thing. It wasn't your fault.'

When I pointed out – as politely as possible – that she actually hated me well before her boyfriend ever dumped her to date me (then went back to her when I, in turn, dumped *him*), she said, while we were sorting through size 36Cs (I'm a 36C!!!! Not a 34B any more!!!! Lana insisted on my getting measured by an actual intimate-apparel expert, and the expert confirmed what I've been suspecting, that I've grown a whole cup size and an inch around as well!), 'Well, it wasn't *you* so much I hated as that jerky friend of yours.'

To which Trisha added, 'Yeah, how can you like that Lilly girl anyway? She's so full of herself.'

I wanted to burst out laughing at that. Because, hello, the Evil-Death Twins, calling LILLY full of herself?

But I started thinking about it, and it IS kind of true, Lilly CAN be a little judgemental and bossy.

But that's why I like her! I mean, at least she HAS opinions about stuff. Stuff that matters anyway. Most of the rest of the people in our class don't care about anything except who wins on *American Idol* and what Ivy League school they get into.

Or, in Lana's case, which shade of lipgloss looks best on her.

But I didn't say anything in Lilly's defence because the truth is, even though I miss her and all – though not so much that it hurts sometimes, the way I do Michael – I need to figure out how to get out of this hole I'm in without the help of the Moscovitzes. Because, as recent developments prove, neither Lilly nor Michael is going to be around to help me when I need them. I've got to learn to stand on my own two feet, without Lilly OR Michael to lean on as emotional crutches.

So I didn't say anything when Lana and Trisha were (mildly) bad-mouthing Lilly. The truth was, I could see their point. It's not like Lilly's ever tried to put herself in Lana's size eight Manolos and seen what it's like to be Lana.

But I have.

And the view from Lana's size eights? It's not all it's cracked up to be.

Don't get me wrong, she's gorgeous, and every guy in the store who wasn't gay (of which there were approximately two) followed her around with his gaze like he couldn't help it.

And she's a SUPER-MEGA-EXCELLENT shopper – I mean, I would never in my life have tried on a pair of Citizens of Humanity jeans. Because Paris Hilton wears them, and even though I don't know Paris personally, she doesn't seem to do a lot for charities or the environment, that I'm aware of.

But Lana insisted they would look good on me and made me try on a pair and so I did and . . .

I look AWESOME in them!!!

And don't even get me started on what a difference

having the right size/style bra makes. In my Agent Provocateur demi-cup underwires, I actually have breasts now. Like breasts that balance out the rest of my body so I don't look pear-shaped or like a Q-tip. I actually look *curvy*.

And, OK, not like Scarlett Johansson curvy.

But like Jessica Biel curvy.

With each Marc Jacobs baby-doll top Lana threw over my arm and commanded me to try on, I began to feel less and less like this whole thing was a trick, and more and more like Lana really was trying to make amends for past wrongs and really did want me to look good. Every time she or Trisha made me try on something – like a faux tiger-fur miniskirt or a gold Rachel Lee link hip-belt – and they went, 'Oh yeah, that's hot,' or, 'No, that's not you, take it off,' I felt like . . . well, like they cared.

And I will admit, it felt good. I didn't feel like it was fake, or like I was Katie Holmes and they were Tom Cruise's Scientologist friends love-bombing me, because there was plenty of, 'Oh my God, Mia, you can NEVER wear red. OK? Promise me. Because you look like crap in it,' to ground me.

It was just . . . girl stuff. The kind of thing Lilly would have totally looked down on. She'd have been all, 'Oh my God, how many bras do you *need*? No one's ever going to see them, so what's the *point*? Especially when so many people are starving in Darfur,' and, 'Why are you buying jeans that have HOLES in them? The point is that you're supposed to wear your OWN holes into your jeans, not buy a pair someone ELSE already made holes in.' And, 'Oh my God, you're getting one of THOSE TOPS? THOSE TOPS are made in sweatshops by little Guatemalan children who are only paid five cents an hour, just so you know.'

Which isn't even true, because Bendel's doesn't carry products made in sweatshops. At least, none of the ladies at the trunk show do. I asked.

And seriously, it wasn't like Lana and Trisha and I ran out of things to talk about. They were like, 'So are you going out with that J.P. guy or what?' and I was like, 'No, we're just friends,' and they were like, 'Well, he's pretty cute. Except for the thing with the corn.'

And then I explained about Michael and I having just broken up and how I feel completely empty inside, like someone shovelled out the inside of my chest with an ice-cream scoop and threw the contents out on the West Side Highway, like a dead hooker.

And they didn't even think that was weird. Lana went, 'Yeah, that's how I felt when Josh dumped me for you,' and I was like, 'Oh my God, I'm so sorry,' and Lana went, 'Whatever. I got over it. And you will too.'

Even though she's wrong. I'll never get over Michael. Not in a million trillion years.

But I'm trying (if you call putting all his letters, cards, photos and gifts in a plastic I ♡ NY shopping bag and stuffing it as far under my bed as it would go last night trying to get over him. I couldn't bring myself to throw them away. I just couldn't).

Anyway, it was . . . surprisingly normal, talking to Lana and Trisha. It was a lot like the way Tina and I talk to each other. Only with thongs (which by the way are pretty comfortable if you get the right size).

And, OK, Lana and Trisha have never read *Jane Eyre* (and gave me a funny look when I mentioned it as being

113

my favourite book of all time) or seen *Buffy* ('Is that the one with the girl from *The Grudge*?').

But they aren't bad people. I think they're more . . . misunderstood. Like, their obsession with eyeliner could very well be taken for shallowness, but it's really just that they're not very curious about the world around them. Unless it has to do with shoes.

And I sort of feel sorry for them – for Lana, at least – because when it came time to ring up what we were buying and Lana's bill came to $1,847.56, and Trisha inhaled and went, 'Dude, your mom is going to KILL you,' since Lana had been given a thousand-dollar spending limit, Lana just shrugged and went, 'Whatever. If she says anything I'll just bring up Bubbles,' and I was like, 'Bubbles?' and Lana looked all sad and went, 'Bubbles was my pony,' and I was like, '*Was?*'

And then Lana explained that when, at age thirteen, she grew too heavy and long-legged for tiny Bubbles to carry her, her parents sold her beloved pony without telling her, thinking a swift and thorough break, with no time for goodbyes, would be less emotionally traumatic.

'They were wrong,' Lana said, handing over her credit card to the sales girl to pay for her charges. 'I don't think I ever got over it. I still miss that fat-assed little horse.'

Which. You know. Harsh. At least Grandmere's never done THAT to me.

Anyway, I guess I should get back to our table. We're treating ourselves to a ladies-who-lunch smorgasbord . . . the Nobu chef's special. It's 'only' a hundred dollars per person.

But Trisha says we're worth it. And besides which it's almost all protein, being raw fish.

Of course, Lana and Trisha just have to pay for themselves. I have to pay for Lars too. And he's having a steak, because he says raw fish saps his man strength.

Saturday, September 18, 6 p.m., Limo on the way to Tina's

When I walked into the loft after shopping Mom was already mad. That's because I had Bendel's concierge service deliver (and also Saks, where we stopped later to pick up some boots and shoes) my shopping bags so I didn't have to carry them around all day, and they were stacked so high in my room that Fat Louie couldn't get around them to get to his litter box in my bathroom.

'HOW MUCH DID YOU SPEND?' Mom wanted to know. Her eyes were all crazy.

It's true there WERE a lot of bags. Rocky had been having a good time ramming the lowest tier with his trucks, trying to make them all fall down. Fortunately, it's hard to damage lycra.

'Relax,' I said. 'I used that black American Express card Dad gave me.'

'THAT CREDIT CARD IS FOR EMERGENCIES ONLY!' Mom practically screamed.

'Hello,' I said. 'You don't think my NEW SIZE THIRTY-SIX C BOOBS count as an emergency?'

So then Mom's lips got all small and she went, 'I don't think Lana Weinberger is a good influence on you. I'm calling your father,' and off she stomped.

Parents. Seriously. First they get on my case because I won't get out of bed or do anything. Then I do what they want, and get out of bed and socialize, and they get mad about THAT too.

You can't win.

While Mom was off ratting me out to Dad (and whatever, OK, I did spend a lot, way more than Lana. But except for ballgowns and the occasional pair of over-alls, I haven't bought clothes in like three years, so they need to get over it), I started stuffing my old, non-fitting clothes into trash bags to take to Good Will, and hanging up my new, totally stylish clothes, plus packing for going to Tina's tonight.

Which I was kind of surprised to find I was looking forward to doing. Lana and Trisha had invited me to some party they were going to at an Upper West Side apartment, given by a senior whose parents were at a spa for the weekend working on their chi. But I told them I already had other plans.

'Launching a new yacht or something?' Lana asked all sarcastically.

Only by now I knew not to take every little thing she said so literally and straight to heart. Most of the time when she makes her little barbs she's just trying to be funny. Even if the only person her remark is funny to is herself. In fact, Lana's a lot like Lilly in that way.

'No, just hanging out with Tina Hakim Baba,' I said, and left it at that. And neither of them seemed offended that I was blowing off the 'party of the semester' to be with a non It-Crowd member.

I was just stuffing my toothbrush into my overnight case when my mom walked in and held out the phone to me.

'Your father wants to speak to you,' she said, and then turned around and walked out, looking smug.

Seriously. I love my mom and all. But she can't have it both ways. She can't raise me to be a socially conscious rebel and then get worried when the weight of my depression about the world oppresses me to the point that I can no longer get out of bed, send me to

117

therapy, then freak out when I follow that therapist's advice. She just can't.

And OK Dr K didn't actually TELL me to spend that much on underwear. But whatever.

'I'm not taking any of it back,' I say to my dad.

'I'm not asking you to,' he said.

'Do you know how much I spent?' I asked suspiciously.

'I do. The credit card company already called me. They thought the card had been stolen and some teenage girl was on a spending spree. Since you've never spent that much before.'

'Oh,' I said. 'Then what did you want to talk to me about?'

'Nothing. I just have to make it seem like I'm yelling at you. You know how your mother is. She's from the Midwest. She can't help it. If it costs more than twenty dollars, she breaks out into hives. She's always been that way.'

'Oh,' I said. Then I added, 'But, Dad. It's not fair!'

'What's not fair?' he wanted to know.

'Nothing,' I said, lowering my voice. 'I'm just pretending like you're yelling at me.'

'Oh,' he said, sounding impressed. 'Good job. Oh no.'

'Oh no, what?'

'Your grandmother just walked in.' Dad sounded tense. 'She wants to talk to you.'

'About how much I spent?' I was surprised. To Grandmere, the amount I paid today at Bendel's equals only a small fraction of what she spends every week on hair and beauty treatments alone.

'Uh, not exactly,' Dad said.

And the next thing I knew, Grandmere was breathing into the phone.

'Amelia,' she snapped. 'What is this your father tells me about our princess lessons being cancelled for the foreseeable future because you have some kind of personal crisis you need to work out?'

'Mother,' I heard Dad yelping in the background. 'That is *not* what I said!'

I knew exactly what was going on. Dad had been trying to get me out of princess lessons with Grandmere without telling Grandmere WHY I needed to miss princess lessons – in other words, without telling her I'm in therapy. With a cowboy psychologist.

'Quiet, Philippe,' Grandmere snapped. 'Don't you think you've done enough?' To me, she said, 'Amelia, this isn't like you. Falling apart because of That Boy? Have I taught you NOTHING? A woman needs a man like a fish needs a bicycle! And whatnot. Pull yourself together!'

'Grandmere,' I said wearily. 'It's not – it's not JUST because of Michael, OK? Things are just kind of stressful for me right now. You know I missed a bunch of school this week, I have tons of work to make up, so if it's OK, I'd really like to take a rain check on princess lessons until—'

'WHAT ABOUT THE DOMINA REIS?' Grandmere shrieked.

'What about them?' I asked.

'We have to start working on your speech!'

'Grandmere, about that, I just don't know if I—'

'Oh no. You are NOT getting out of this, Amelia. Not this time. You agreed—'

'But that was back when I still thought there was a chance Michael and I might get back together. Everything was different then. *I* was different then—'

'You are giving this speech, Amelia,' Grandmere barked, 'and that's final. I already told them you would. And I already BRAGGED about it to the Contessa! Now, tomorrow afternoon, you are meeting me at the Genovian Embassy, and together we shall pore over the royal archives for some kind of material that will hopefully inspire your speech. Is that understood?'

'But, Grandmere—'

'Tomorrow. The Embassy. Two o'clock.'

Click!

Well. I guess she told me.

And I guess my dream of spending all day Sunday in bed has been crushed.

Mom just poked her head in here. She seems to have gotten over her rage about my spendaholism. She was chewing her lower lip and going, 'Mia, I'm sorry. But I had to do it. Do you realize you spent almost as much as the gross national product of a small developing nation . . . only you spent it on low-rise jeans?'

'Yeah,' I said, trying to look sorry. Which wasn't hard, because I *am* sorry.

Sorry I never bought jeans like that before. Because I look HOT in them.

Besides, what Mom doesn't know – nor Dad, yet – is that while Lana and Trisha and I were eating, I called Amnesty International and donated the exact amount I spent at Bendel's, using the emergency black Amex.

So I don't even feel guilty. That much.

'I know things are bad right now with Michael, and with you and Lilly,' Mom went on. 'And I'm glad you're trying to make new friends. I'm just not sure Lana Weinberger is the RIGHT friend for you . . .'

'She's not that bad, Mom,' I said, thinking of the

pony thing. And also the other thing Lana told me over lunch. Which is that her mom told her that if she doesn't get into an Ivy League school, she's not going to pay for her to go college ANYWHERE. Talk about harsh.

'And it's so unfair,' Lana had said. 'Because it's not like I'm smart, like you are, Mia.'

I'd nearly choked on my wasabi at that one. *'Me? Smart?'*

'Yeah,' Trisha had added. 'AND you're a princess, which means you're going to get in everywhere you apply no matter what. Because everyone wants royalty at their school.'

Ouch. Also, true.

'Well, Mia,' Mom said, looking dubious – I guess about my remark that Lana Weinberger is not that bad, 'I'm happy you're keeping an open mind and are a little more willing to try new things than you've been in the past –' I don't even know what she could mean by that, unless she's talking about meat and its by-products – 'but remember the golden rule.'

'You mean that in a good bra your nipple should fall exactly midway between your shoulder and elbow?'

'Um,' Mom said, looking long-suffering. 'No. I meant *Make new friends, but keep the old. One is silver and the other gold.'*

'Oh,' I said. 'Yeah, right. Don't worry. I'm going to go spend the night at Tina's now. See ya.'

Then I got out of there. And none too soon either, because I was really afraid she was going to notice my chandelier earrings, which cost as much as Rocky's stroller.

Saturday, September 18, 9 p.m., Tina Hakim Baba's bathroom

I'm really glad I agreed to spend the night at Tina's tonight. Even though I am still pretty much morbidly depressed, Tina's house is my third favourite place to be (the first being Michael's arms, of course, and the second being my bed).

So being at Tina's isn't at all excruciating, like being at, say, Bendel's during a lingerie trunk show.

Although I've still told Tina nothing of my current emotional state – like that I feel as if I'm at the bottom of a hole and can't find my way out, etc. – she has been more than supportive about my fashion transformation, complimenting my earrings, telling me that my butt looks really good in my new jeans, and even asking me if I'd LOST weight . . . not *gained* it!

That, of course, is the result of a fantastically supportive – and also a little bit padded, for extra nipple-erection camouflage – well-fitted bra.

The first thing we did (after we ordered two pepperoni pizzas with extra cheese and ate them) was change all the clocks so that her siblings thought it was bedtime, then put them to bed, ignoring their plaintive protests that they were not tired. They wept themselves to sleep soon enough.

Then we broke out the DVDs and got to work. Tina has composed the following flow chart so we can keep track of Drew Barrymore's body of work, which, as Tina insists, is important, because one day Drew will be a star along the lines of a Meryl Streep or Dame Judi

Dench, and we'll want to be able to discourse knowledgeably about her oeuvre.

Drew Barrymore: The Important Works

Curious George –
Tina: I never saw this.
Mia: Whatever, it's for babies!
0 out of 5 gold Drews

Fever Pitch –
Tina: Excellent, classic Drew. Works well with Jimmy Fallon.
Mia: Too much stuff about baseball.
Tina: Well, that's kind of the point.
3 out of 5 gold Drews

50 First Dates –
Tina: Never quite reaches the comic pitch of *The Wedding Singer*, the last film in which Drew was paired with Adam Sandler.
Mia: Still, funny.
3 out of 5 gold Drews

Duplex –
Tina: It pains me that Drew was in this movie.
Mia: I know. It hurts me deep inside. Still, she's Drew, so . . .
1 out of 5 gold Drews

Charlie's Angels: Full Throttle –
Tina: Awesome, butt-kicking Drew!
Mia: Not sure what all the hand-holding with Lucy Liu

and Cameron was about during the press junkets for this film.

Tina: Right. Who holds hands with their *girl* friends?

Mia: Except Spencer and Ashley on *South of Nowhere*, of course. But they're dating.

Tina: Which is totally different.

Mia: Still.

5 out of 5 gold Drews

Confessions of a Dangerous Mind –

Tina: My parents wouldn't let me see this movie. It was rated R.

Mia: I didn't WANT to see this movie. It has old people in it. But she's Drew, so . . .

1 out of 5 gold Drews

Riding in Cars with Boys –

Tina: Did you see this movie?

Mia: No. I never heard of it.

Tina: But it was probably good.

Mia: If Drew was in it, of course.

1 out of 5 gold Drews

Donnie Darko –

Tina: Wait – Drew was in this movie?

Mia: I totally don't remember her. All I remember was Jake.

Tina: I know. He was so hot in this.

Mia: Let's give it a high score for Jake.

Tina: Totally. And my parents won't let me see *Brokeback* or *Jarhead*.

5 out of 5 gold Drews

Never Been Kissed –

Tina: SO AWESOME!!! DREW IS SO CUTE IN THIS!!!

Mia: I know! She's a reporter AND a high-school student!!! She should have to play a high-school student in EVERY MOVIE SHE'S IN.

5 out of 5 gold Drews

Home Fries –

Tina: I don't remember this movie except that she had curly hair.

Mia: Wasn't she pregnant or something?

Tina: So the curls definitely weren't a perm. Because that could hurt the baby.

Mia: The curls were cute, so let's give it a high score.

4 out of 5 gold Drews

Ever After –

Tina: Best movie ever.

Mia: Agreed. When she carries the prince –

Tina: Shut up!!! I LOVE THAT PART!!!!

Mia: Just –

Tina: – breathe! EEEEE!

5,000,000 out of 5 gold Drews

The Wedding Singer –

Tina: Drew looks so cute in her waitress outfit.

Mia: I know! And when he sings that bad song –

Tina: – she's still nice to him.

5 out of 5 gold Drews

Bad Girls –

Tina: This movie is so bad it's kind of good.

Mia: I know. But I think when Drew is captured and they tie to her the bed and she's face down –

Tina: It's called Turkish style.

Mia: Whoever says romance novels aren't educational is a liar.

4 out of 5 gold Drews

The Amy Fisher Story –

Tina: Drew is not too proud to do made-for-TV movies! And she plays a homicidal Long Island teen!

Mia: Brilliantly, I might add.

5 out of 5 gold Drews

Irreconcilable Differences –

Tina: A very young Drew in a very cute role!

Mia: Love it. Love her.

4 out of 5 gold Drews

Firestarter –

Tina: I know you love this movie, so I'm not going to say anything.

Mia: Shut up! How can you not like it? She's so good!

Tina: She's extraordinary for her age. It's just . . . the story is so silly!

Mia: People can totally start fires with their minds if they're emotional enough. Look what you keep saying about J.P.

Tina: True.

4 out of 5 gold Drews

E.T. the Extra-Terrestrial –

Tina: She's so cute in this!

Mia: And such a good actress. It's like she's ad-libbing her lines, they come so naturally.

Tina: Face it. Drew's a genius. I wish she'd get her own talk show.

Mia: I wish she'd run for president.

Tina: President Barrymore! YEAH!!!!

5 out of 5 gold Drews

We are taking a break now between *The Wedding Singer* and *Ever After*, while Tina makes popcorn. During the boring non-Drew parts of *The Wedding Singer*, Tina asked me if I'd heard anything from Michael, so I told her about his email, and she was rightfully indignant on my behalf. I mean, that Michael would try to pretend like we were just friends and tell me about his egg-sandwich-finding hardships and not tell me instead how much he misses me or how much he wishes we could get back together.

But then I pointed out to Tina that I'd agreed to just be friends. Also that the whole thing was my fault in the first place for blowing up over the Judith Gershner Affair, instead of playing it cool, the way Drew would have.

Which Tina was forced to concede was true. She also agreed that it was good I hadn't written back.

'Because you don't want to seem like you're sitting around at home with nothing better to do than answer emails from your ex-boyfriend,' she said.

Even if that's actually true.

Although it's not really. I feel kind of guilty not telling Tina about how I spent my day – you know, with Lana and Trisha. I don't know why. I mean, Grandmere has pointed out a million times that it's totally rude to tell someone about an outing on which you went but to which they were not themselves invited. So there's no reason I SHOULD tell Tina about Lana and Trisha.

Still. It was LANA.

I –

What's THAT? I think I just heard Tina's doorman buzz up that there's someone in the lobby –

Sunday, September 19, 2 a.m., Tina Hakim Baba's bedroom

Oh. My. God.

So Tina was just finishing pouring melted butter over the low-fat microwave popcorn to make it actually taste like something when the doorman announced that Boris and 'a friend' were down in the lobby.

Tina flipped out, of course, because she's not supposed to have boys over when her parents aren't home.

But Boris got on the intercom and said he was only dropping something off, a present for us. So of course Tina couldn't resist letting them come up. Because, as she put it, 'Present!!!!!'

But if you ask me the present was just an excuse so that Boris could come up and make out with Tina. Because all the 'present' was was a couple of containers of Häagen-Dazs (to be honest, they were our favourite flavours, vanilla swiss almond and macadamia brittle. But still).

The real surprise – at least to me – was that the 'friend' turned out to be J.P.

I didn't even know J.P. and Boris hung out that much. I mean, outside the lunchroom.

J.P. looked shockingly . . . well, *good* as he followed Boris into Tina's apartment. I don't know what he's done to himself, but he looks all tall and . . . *guy* like.

The thing is, I don't normally notice this kind of thing about any guy except Michael. I don't know what's the matter with me. Maybe it was just the shock of seeing J.P. in a setting outside school, or in jeans

129

instead of his school uniform or theatre-going clothes. Maybe it's just all the comments from people, telling me how hot J.P. is, rubbing off on me.

Or maybe I'm just hot-guy deprived, on account of not having had Michael around for so long or something.

Still, it was weird.

J.P., in addition to looking hot, looked kind of abashed too. He shuffled in and said, 'Hi,' to me, while Tina was squealing over the ice cream and running to get spoons.

Tina is not the hardest person to please when it comes to presents. Case in point, she will practically faint over anything from Kay Jewelers.

'Hi,' I said back. And I don't know why (well, I do know why: it was the hot thing), but it was weird. I guess mainly it was weird because J.P. had asked me what I was doing tonight and I'd sort of blown him off and . . . well, there we were together.

But also because of the hot thing.

And things got progressively weirder. Because at first things were cool, and we were all eating the ice cream and watching *Ever After* (Tina told the guys they could stay for ONE movie, but then they had to go, because if her parents found them there, they'd kill her. Well, her dad would anyway. He'd probably kill Boris too, and in a particularly painful way he'd learned from Tina's bodyguard, Wahim, who'd been given the night off, along with Lars, since they'd been informed we were 'in' for the evening).

But then Tina and Boris stopped paying attention to the movie and started paying attention to each other. A LOT of attention. Like, basically their tongues were in one another's mouths. Right in front of J.P. and me! Which wasn't TOO embarrassing (not).

After a while I couldn't take the slurping noises any more (although I kept turning up the volume of the TV. But even Drew's pseudo British accent couldn't drown out those two).

So finally I grabbed the melting ice-cream containers and said, 'Somebody should put these in the freezer before they make a mess,' and jumped up to leave the room.

Unfortunately – or maybe fortunately, I don't know – J.P. said, 'I'll help you,' and followed me. Even though how hard is it to return two ice-cream containers to the freezer? I totally could have done it by myself.

Inside the Hakim Babas' cool, clean kitchen, with its black granite counters and Sub-Zero appliances, J.P. grabbed a root beer from the fridge, then pulled out a kitchen-counter stool and slid on to it while I fought to find space in the crowded freezer for the ice cream. There were a LOT of Healthy Choice frozen dinners in there (Tina's dad is supposed to be watching his calories and cholesterol).

'So,' J.P. said, conversationally. In the background, we could hear the television from the media room, but not, thank God, the slurping noises any more. 'You missed a lot of school last week.'

'Uh,' I said, as I wrestled with what looked like a frozen beef tenderloin. 'Yeah. I guess I did.'

'How are you doing now?' J.P. wanted to know. 'I mean, you must have a lot of make-up work.'

'Yeah,' I said. The truth is, I've barely looked at all that. When you're sunk as deep in a hole as I am, homework doesn't seem all that important. Not as

131

important as new jeans anyway. 'I'll get to it tomorrow, I guess.'

'Yeah? What'd you do today then?'

I was so busy jamming the meat deeper into the freezer that I didn't even think about my reply. 'I went shopping with Lana,' I said with a grunt. Then, FINALLY, the meat gave way, and I was able to slide the ice cream into the freezer.

It wasn't until I slammed the freezer door shut and turned round, brushing ice shards off my hands, that I saw J.P.'s expression and realized what I'd just admitted.

'Lana?' he echoed incredulously.

I glanced towards the hallway to the media room. Empty, fortunately. Boris and Tina were still, um, occupied.

'Uh,' I said, feeling my stomach lurch. *What had I done?* 'Yeah. About that . . . I don't know where that came from. I wasn't going to tell anybody.'

'I can see why,' J.P. said. 'I mean, LANA? On the other hand, is she the one who picked out that shirt?'

I looked down at the silky baby-doll top I was wearing. I'll admit, it was pretty cute. And low cut.

And, amazingly, with one of my new bras – and my new chest size – I actually had a tiny bit of cleavage in it. Nothing trashy, but definitely *there*.

'Uh, yeah,' I said, feeling myself blush. 'Lana's a really good shopper . . .' Which might just about be the lamest thing I have ever said. And I mean ever.

But J.P. just nodded and went, 'I can see that. I think she's found her calling. But how on earth did THAT happen?'

Hesitantly, I told him about the Domina Reis, and

how Lana's mother had asked me to speak at that this Domina Rei event she's in charge of, and how Lana had thanked me for agreeing to do so, and how one thing led to another, and . . .

'I get all that,' J.P. said when I was done. 'I mean, I can see Lana asking you to go shopping with her. She's wanted to get in good with you for years. But why did you say YES?'

I don't really know how to explain what happened next. I mean, why I said what I did. Maybe it was because it was just the two of us in the Hakim Babas' quiet kitchen (well, quiet except for the dishwasher, cleaning our pizza plates. But it was one of those super-silent ones that just went *swish-swish* all softly).

Maybe it was because J.P. looked so out of place sitting there – this big raw-boned-looking guy in this fancy kitchen, with the sleeves of his charcoal cashmere sweater shoved up to his elbows, and his faded jeans and Timberlands, and his hair kind of sticking up in tufts because he'd been wearing a hat outside. We're having a surprisingly cold snap, for September. The meteorologists all blame global warming.

Or maybe it was the hot thing again – that, you know, he did look . . . well, pretty cute.

Or maybe it's just that I DON'T *know* him – at least, not as well as I know Tina and Boris and the other friends I have left, now that Lilly's no longer speaking to me.

Whatever it was, suddenly, before I could stop myself, I heard myself going, 'Well, you see, the thing is, I'm in therapy, and my therapist says I have to do something every day that scares me. And I thought shopping with Lana Weinberger would be really scary. Only it turned out it wasn't.'

Then I bit my lip. Because, you know. That's a lot to unload on someone. Especially a guy. Especially a guy with whom you've been romantically linked in the press, even if there is absolutely, categorically, no truth to the rumours whatsoever.

J.P. didn't say anything right away. He just sat there peeling the label off his bottle of root beer with his thumbnail. He seemed really interested in the level of liquid left in the bottle.

Which wasn't the best sign, you know? Like that he couldn't even look at me.

'It's weird,' I said, feeling totally panicky all of a sudden. Like I was slipping further down that hole than ever. 'It's weird that I just admitted I'm in therapy to you, isn't it? You think I'm a freak now. Right? I mean, a bigger freak than before.'

But instead of making up an excuse about how he had to go now, as I expected him to, J.P. looked up from his bottle in surprise. And smiled.

And I felt the sliding sensation I was experiencing subside a little. And not just because the smile made him look cuter than ever.

'Are you kidding me?' he asked. 'I was just wondering if there's any kid at Albert Einstein who ISN'T in therapy. Besides Tina and Boris, I mean.'

I blinked at him. 'Wait . . . you too?'

J.P. snorted. 'Since I was twelve. Well, that's when I developed this total affinity for dropping bottles off the roof of our high-rise. It was a stupid thing to do . . . somebody could have gotten killed. Eventually I got caught – deservedly so – and my parents have seen to it that I haven't missed a weekly session since.'

I couldn't believe this. Someone else I knew was going through the same thing I was? No way.

I slid on to the kitchen stool next to J.P.'s and asked eagerly, 'Do you have to do something that scares you every day too?'

'Uh,' J.P. said. 'No. I'm supposed to do FEWER scary things every day actually.'

'Oh,' I said, feeling vaguely disappointed. 'Well. Is it working?'

'Lately,' J.P. said. He took a sip of his root beer. 'Lately it's been working great. Do you want one of these?'

I shook my head. 'How long did it take?' I asked eagerly. This was amazing. I couldn't believe I was actually talking to someone who'd been through – was going through – the same thing I was. Or something similar anyway. 'I mean, before you started feeling better? Before it started working?'

J.P. looked at me with a funny smile on his face. It took me a minute before I realized it was pitying. He felt *sorry* for me.

'That bad, huh?' he asked. Not in a mean way. Like he genuinely felt bad for me.

But that's not what I want. I don't want anyone to feel bad for me. I mean, it's stupid I even feel so awful about everything, when, in general, I have a fantastic life. I mean look at what Lana has to put up with – a mother who sold her beloved pony without even telling her, and a threat that if she doesn't get into an Ivy League she can kiss her parents' financial support goodbye. I'm a PRINCESS, for crying out loud. I can do whatever I want. I can *buy* whatever I want. Well, within reason. The one thing – the *one thing* – I don't have is the man I love.

And it's my own stupid fault that I lost him in the first place.

'I've just been a little down,' I said quickly. I didn't mention the part about not wanting to get out of bed all week.

'Michael?' J.P. asked. Not without compassion.

I nodded. I didn't think I could have spoken if I'd wanted to. This big lump had formed in my throat, the way it always does when I hear – when I even *think* – his name.

But it turned out I didn't have to speak. J.P. let go of the root-beer bottle and put his hand on mine.

I sort of wish he hadn't though. Because that just made me feel more like crying than ever. Because I couldn't help comparing his hand – which was large and guy-like, but not quite as large and guy-like – to someone else's.

'Hey,' he said softly, giving my fingers a squeeze. 'It gets better. I promise.'

'Really?' I asked. It was too late now. The tears were coming. I tried to choke them back as best I could. 'It's not just . . . just Michael, you know,' I heard myself assuring him. Because I didn't want anyone to think I was depressed just because of a boy. Even if that really was the truth. 'I mean, there's the whole thing with Lilly. I can't believe she really thinks you and I – that you and I would ever—'

'Hey,' J.P. said, looking a little alarmed, I think at how thick and fast my tears were coming. 'Hey.'

And the next thing I knew, he had wrapped me in his

big bear-like embrace, and I was weeping on to the front of his sweater. Which smelt like dry-cleaning fluid.

A fact that actually just made me weep harder, when I remembered that I would never again get to smell the one thing that I miss and love more than any other . . . Michael's neck.

Which definitely does not smell of dry-cleaning fluid.

'Shhh,' J.P. said, patting me on the back while I cried. 'It's going to be OK. It really is.'

'I don't see how,' I sobbed. 'Lilly hates me! She won't even look at me!'

'Well, maybe that should tell you something,' J.P. said.

'Tell me what?' I hiccuped against his chest. 'That she hates me? I already know that.'

'No,' J.P. said. 'That maybe she's not as great a friend as you've always thought she was.'

This actually caused me to stop crying and sit back and blink at him tearfully.

'Wh-what do you mean?' I asked.

'Well, just that if she really was as good a friend as you seem to think,' J.P. said, 'she wouldn't believe that there's anything going on between you and me. Because she'd know you aren't capable of something like that. She certainly wouldn't be mad at you for something you didn't even do – despite maybe a little evidence to the contrary. I mean, did she even bother asking you if that thing in the *Post* about us was true?'

I dabbed at the corners of my eyes with a napkin J.P. pulled out of a nearby holder and handed to me.

'No,' I said.

'I haven't had a lot of friends,' J.P. said. 'I'll admit it. But I still don't think friends treat each other that way

– just believe something they read or hear without even confirming whether or not it's really true. Right? I mean, what kind of friend does that?'

'I know,' I said with a last, shuddering little sob. 'You're right.'

'Look,' J.P. said. 'I know you've been friends with her forever, Mia. But there's a lot of stuff about Lilly I don't think you know. Stuff she told me when we were going out that – well, I mean, for instance, she was always pretty jealous of you.'

I stared at him, totally astonished.

'What are you TALKING about?' I cried. 'Why on earth would Lilly ever be jealous of ME?'

'For the same reason I imagine a lot of girls – including Lana Weinberger – are jealous of you. You're pretty, you're smart, you're popular, you're a princess, everyone likes you—'

'WHAT?' I was laughing now. In disbelief. But still. It was better than crying. 'I look like a Q-tip! And I'm flunking half my classes! And MOST of the people in school think I'm nothing but a five foot nine, I mean ten, flat-chested freak—'

'Maybe some of them used to think that,' J.P. said, smiling at me. 'And maybe to some of them, you used to seem that way. But, Mia, you need to take a good look at yourself in the mirror. You aren't that person any more. And maybe that's what Lilly's problem is. You've changed . . . and she hasn't.'

'That . . . that's ridiculous,' I said. 'I'm still the same old Mia—'

'Who eats meat and goes shopping with Lana Weinberger,' J.P. pointed out. 'Face it, Mia. You're not the same person you used to be. That doesn't mean you

138

aren't BETTER, or that there aren't people who are going to love you no matter what you eat or who you hang out with. But not everyone is going to be able to wrap their minds around it the way, say, Tina and I have.'

I blinked at him some more. Could this be true? Could the real reason Lilly wanted nothing to do with me be because, far from being disgusted with me, she's actually jealous of me?

'But that's so absurd!' I finally burst out. 'Lilly's so much smarter and more accomplished than I am. She's a genius, for crying out loud! What could I possibly have that she doesn't? Except a tiara.'

'That's a big part of it,' J.P. said with a shrug. 'The fact that you're a princess *is* really special. I've never understood why you've never thought so. Most people would kill to be royal, and yet you spend all your time wishing you weren't. Not that being royal is *all* that makes you special . . . by any means.'

'If you spent five minutes in my shoes,' I grumbled, 'you'd realize how *not* special being me really is. Believe me. There's not a special bone in my body.'

'Mia,' J.P. said, lifting up one of the hands I'd left lying on the kitchen counter. 'There's something I've been wanting to tell you—'

But it was right at that moment that the doorman buzzed up to let Tina know her parents were in the foyer (good thing Tina regularly slips the guy batches of her home-made chocolate chocolate-chip cookies, so he's totally willing to do her bidding). Tina came barrelling in, looking wild-eyed, yelling that Boris and J.P. had to leave through the servants' entrance RIGHT THEN . . . which they promptly did.

So I never did get to find out what it was J.P. was going to tell me.

After they were gone, and we'd said hi to her parents and gone into Tina's room to get away from them, Tina apologized for having spent so much time in a liplock with Boris.

'It's just,' she said, 'he's so cute, sometimes I can't help myself.'

'It's OK,' I told her. 'I understand.'

'Still,' Tina fretted. 'It was terrible of us to rub how happy we are in your face, when you're still trying to get over Michael. What did you and J.P. end up talking about anyway?'

'Oh,' I said uncomfortably. 'Nothing really.'

Tina looked surprised. 'Because Boris said when he mentioned you were spending the night with me, J.P. wouldn't stop talking about how the two of them had to come over here. Even though Boris explained about my dad's rule. But J.P. kept saying he had something really important he had to tell you, and practically forced Boris to bring him here. Are you *sure* he didn't say anything?'

'Well, we talked about a lot of stuff,' I said. I hate lying to Tina! But I can't tell her we talked about being in therapy. I'm just not ready to admit that to her yet. I know it's stupid – I know she wouldn't judge me. But . . . I just can't. 'You know. Mostly about Lilly.'

'That's interesting,' Tina said. 'You know, Boris thinks J.P.'s in love with you, and I agree. Maybe *that*'s what he wanted to tell.'

I had a good long laugh at that one. Really, the

best laugh I've had since Michael and I broke up. The ONLY laugh I've had since then, really.

But Tina wasn't joking, it turned out.

'Look at the facts, Mia,' she said. 'J.P. dumped Lilly the minute he heard you and Michael had broken up. He dumped her because he's in love with you, and he realized he finally had a chance at getting you, now that you're single.'

'Tina!' I wiped tears from my eyes. 'Come on. Be serious.'

'I *am* serious, Mia. This totally happened in *The Sheik's Secret Baby* . . . and I bet that's why Lilly is so mad at you.'

'Because I gave away the fact that she had the sheik's secret baby?' I couldn't help giggling. It's really hard to feel depressed when you're around Tina. Even when you're trapped at the bottom of a cistern.

Tina looked disappointed in me. 'No. Because she suspects you're the real reason why J.P. dumped her. Because he loves *you*. Which is totally unfair of her, because it's not your fault. You can't help it if guys fall in love with you, any more than the princess in *The Sheik's Secret Baby* could. But still, you have to admit that's totally what happened. It explains EVERY-THING.'

I laughed for like ten more minutes. Seriously, Tina lives in the cutest fantasy world. She really should write her own romance novels for a living. Or do stand-up comedy.

Too bad she wants to be a thoracic surgeon instead.

Sunday, September 19, 5 p.m., the Loft

Hanging out with Grandmere is hardly ever fun.

Hanging out with Grandmere in the Genovian Embassy royal archive room on basically zero sleep is the total OPPOSITE of fun. Whatever is the least fun thing you can think of.

That's what my day today with Grandmere was like.

Don't get me wrong. I am totally interested in the lives of my ancestors.

It's just . . . after a while, all those wars and famines? They kind of start seeming the same.

Still, Grandmere insists the royal archives are where I'm most likely to find material for my speech to the Domina Reis.

'Now, remember, Amelia,' she kept saying. 'You want to INSPIRE them . . . but at the same time, it's important to AWE them. While also INFORMING them, of course. So that they go away feeling that you've fed not just their minds and hearts, but their SOULS as well.'

OK, Grandmere. Whatever you say.

Also, hello, much pressure?

Grandmere, of course, gravitated towards the writings of the more well-known Renaldos, and asked to be brought the complete works of Grandpere.

But I was more interested in some lesser-known works. You know, that maybe I could crib from without crediting, so it seemed like I made it all up myself?

Because I'm *depressed*. That's not exactly a big boon to creativity. Despite what certain songwriters might say.

The guy in charge of the archives – who actually looked a lot like the way I expected Dr Knutz to . . . you know, elderly, bald and goateed – did a lot of gusty exhaling as Grandmere sent him climbing around the files. We don't keep, he tried to explain, ALL the royal writings in the embassy. MOST of them are at the palace. They'd just brought a few tons over when the Genovian Embassy celebrated its fiftieth anniversary a decade ago, and they hadn't had a chance to send them back yet, due to no one having expressed an interest in seeing them since . . .

Grandmere wasn't interested in hearing any of this. Nor was she interested in hearing about why she shouldn't have brought her miniature poodle, Rommel, to the archives room, since animal dander can be harmful to ancient manuscripts. She kept Rommel exactly where he was, on her lap, and said, 'Don't stand there looking like a nutcracker, Monsieur Christophe.' (Which was actually really funny, because he DID look like a nutcracker!) 'Bring us tea. And don't scrimp on the finger sandwiches this time.'

'Finger sandwiches!' Monsieur Christophe cried, looking, if such a thing were possible, even paler than before (which is hard for a guy who clearly spends practically zero time outdoors). 'But, Your Highness, the *manuscripts* . . . were any food or beverage to get on the *manuscripts*, it could—'

'Good heavens, we aren't toddlers, Monsieur Christophe!' Grandmere cried. 'We aren't going to have a food fight! Now, get us the complete writings of my husband before I have to get up and do it myself!'

Off Monsieur Christophe went, looking extremely unhappy and giving Grandmere an excuse to turn her hypercritical eye towards me.

'Good Lord, Amelia,' she said after a minute. 'What are those . . . THINGS in your ear-lobes?'

Crud. I forgot to take out my new chandelier earrings.

'Oh,' I said. 'Those. Yeah. Well, I bought them yesterday—'

'You look like a gypsy,' Grandmere declared. 'Remove them at once. And what on earth is happening with your chest?'

I had tried to go conservative by putting on a Marc Jacobs dress with a Peter Pan collar that Lana assured me was the height of chic urban sophisticate. Especially when paired with brown patterned stockings and platform Mary Janes.

Unfortunately it was what was beneath the brown wool bodice that had Grandmere up in arms.

'I got a new bra,' I said from between gritted teeth.

'I can see that,' Grandmere said. 'I'm not blind. It's what you've stuffed down it that has me confused.'

'Nothing's stuffed down it, Grandmere,' I said, again from between gritted teeth. 'That's all me. I've grown.'

'That will be the day,' Grandmere said.

And before I knew what was happening, she'd reached out and pinched me!

On the boob!

'OW!' I yelled, leaping away from her. 'What is WRONG with you?'

But Grandmere already looked smug.

'You HAVE grown,' she said. 'It must have been all that good Genovian olive oil we pumped you full of this summer—'

'More likely all the harmful hormones with which the USDA pumps their cattle,' I said, massaging my now throbbing boob. 'Since I've started eating meat I've grown an inch in height and another inch – well, everywhere else. So you don't have to pinch me. I guarantee you, it's all real. Also, OW. That really hurt. How would you like it if someone did that to you?'

'We'll make certain Chanel gets your new measurements,' Grandmere said, looking pleased. 'This is wonderful, Mia, finally we'll be able to put you into something strapless – and you'll actually be able to hold it up for a change!'

Seriously. I hate her sometimes.

Monsieur Christophe finally came with the tea and sandwiches . . . and Grandpere's writings. Which were stored in multiple cardboard boxes. And all seemed to be about drainage issues, from which Genovia was suffering during most of his rule.

'I don't want to give a speech about DRAINAGE,' I informed Grandmere. Actually, the truth was, I didn't want to give a speech at all. But since I knew that kind of attitude would get me nowhere – both with Grandmere AND Dr Knutz, who have a lot in common, if you think about it – I settled for whining about the subject matter. 'Grandmere, all these papers . . . they're basically about the Genovian sewage system. I can't talk to the Domina Reis about SEWAGE. Don't you have anything –' I turned to Monsieur Christophe, who was hovering nearby, gasping every time either of us lifted up one of his precious papers – 'more PERSONAL?'

'Don't be ridiculous, Amelia,' Grandmere said. 'You can't read your grandfather's personal papers to the Domina Reis.'

The truth was, of course, I wasn't thinking about

Grandpere. Although he had some nifty correspondence he'd written during the war, I'd been hoping for something by someone a little less . . .

Male? Boring? RECENT?

'What about her?' I asked, pointing to a portrait that was hanging in an alcove above the water cooler. It was actually a very nice little painting of a slightly moon-faced young girl in Renaissance-type clothes, framed elaborately in heavy gold leaf.

'*Her?*' Grandmere all but snorted. 'Never mind *her.*'

'Who is she?' I asked. Mainly to annoy Grandmere, who so clearly wanted to keep on reading about drainage. But also because it was a very pretty picture. And the girl in it looked sad. Like she might not be unfamiliar with the sensation of slipping down a cistern.

'That,' Monsieur Christophe said in a weary tone, 'is Her Royal Highness Amelie Virginie Renaldo, the fifty-seventh princess of Genovia, who ruled in the year sixteen sixty-nine.'

I blinked a few times. Then I looked at Grandmere.

'Why haven't we ever studied her before?' I asked. Because, believe me, Grandmere has made me memorize my ancestral line. And nowhere is there an Amelie Virginie on it. Amelie is a very popular name in Genovia, because it's the name of the patron saint of the country, a young peasant girl who saved the principality from a marauding invader by lulling him to sleep with a plaintive song, then lopping his head off.

'Because she only ruled for twelve days,' Grandmere said impatiently, 'before dying of the bubonic plague.'

'She DID?' I couldn't help it. I jumped up out of my

seat and hurried over to the water cooler to look at the little portrait. 'She looks like she's MY age!'

'She was,' Grandmere said in a tired voice. 'Amelia, would you please sit down? We don't have time for this. The gala is in less than a week, we need to come up with a speech for you *now*—'

'Oh my God, this is so sad.' I guess one of the symptoms of being depressed is that you basically just cry all the time. Because I was fully welling up. Princess Amelie Virginie was so pretty, like Madonna back before she went macrobiotic and got all into the Kabbalah and weightlifting and still had chubby cheeks and stuff. She looked a little bit like Lilly in a way. If Lilly was a brunette. And wore a crown and a blue velvet choker. 'What was she, like, sixteen?'

'Indeed.' Monsieur Christophe had come to stand beside me. 'It was a terrible time to be alive. The plague was decimating not just the countryside, but the royal court as well. She lost both her parents and all her brothers to it. That's how she inherited the throne. She only ruled for, as Her Highness said, twelve days before succumbing to the plague herself. But during that time she made some decisions – controversial those days – that ultimately saved many Genovians, if not the entire coastal populace . . . including closing the Port of Genovia to all incoming and outgoing ship traffic, and shutting the palace gates against all visitors . . . even the physicians who might have been able to save her. But she didn't want to risk the disease spreading further to her people.'

'Oh my God,' I said, laying a hand on my chest and trying not to sob. 'That is so sad! Where are her writings?'

Monsieur Christophe blinked up at me (because in my platform Mary Janes, I was like six feet two, and he was just a little guy – like Grandmere said, a nutcracker). 'I beg your pardon, Your Highness?'

'Her writings,' I said. 'Princess Amelie Virginie's. I'd like to see them.'

'For God's sake, Amelia,' Grandmere burst out, looking as if she could really use a Sidecar and a cigarette, and not the tea and finger sandwiches (without mayo) to which she'd been relegated by her doctor. 'She doesn't have any writings! She was dealing with a plague! She didn't have time to write anything! She was too busy having the bodies of her maids burned in the palace courtyard.'

'Actually,' Monsieur Christophe said thoughtfully, 'she kept a journal—'

'DO NOT GET THE JOURNAL,' Grandmere leaped up to say. As she did so, she dislodged Rommel, who went plunging to the floor, where he skittered around, trying to find his balance, before retiring gloomily to a far corner of the room. 'WE DO NOT HAVE TIME FOR THIS!'

'Get the journal,' I said to Monsieur Christophe. 'I want to read it.'

'Actually,' the archivist said. 'We have a translation of it. Since it was written in seventeenth-century French, and it was, of course, so short – only twelve days – we started on a translation, only to discover they did not turn out to be twelve particularly, er, important days of Genovian history. Just from a glance at the first few pages, one can see that the Princess does seem to write quite a bit about missing her cat –'

That's when I knew I HAD to read it.

'I want to see the translation,' I said just as Grandmere cried, 'Amelia, SIT DOWN!'

Monsieur Christophe hesitated, clearly not knowing what to do. On the one hand, I'm closer in line to the throne than Grandmere is. On the other hand, she's louder and way scarier.

'You know what?' I whispered to Monsieur Christophe. 'I'll call you later.'

Only I didn't. As soon as I got out of there and into the safety of my limo, I called Dad and told him what I wanted.

If he thought it was strange, he didn't say anything about it. Although I guess my taking an interest in anything that doesn't involve my bed must seem like an improvement to him.

Anyway, when I got home, there was a package waiting for me. Dad had had Monsieur Christophe messenger over not just the translation of Princess Amelie Virginie's journal, but her portrait as well.

Which I've leaned against the wall at the end of my bed, where my TV used to be. She perfectly covers up the ugly cable outlet, and I can see her from any angle when I'm in bed.

Which I'm in right now.

Because they can take away my television.

And they can throw away my Hello Kitty pyjamas.

And they can make me go to school and to therapy.

But they can't keep me out of my own bed!

(Although I have to say my own problems pale in comparison to poor Princess Amelie Virginie's. I mean, at least I don't have the PLAGUE.)

Sunday, September 19, 11 p.m., the Loft

I just realized it's been exactly a week since I got that phone call from Michael letting me know it's all over between us. I mean, except as friends.

I really don't know what to say about that. A part of me still wants to crawl into bed and just cry forever of course, even though you would think by now I'd be all cried out (although whenever I think about how I'll never feel his arms around me again, the tears come welling right back up).

But then I think about how many people have it worse than me. Princess Amelie Virginie, for instance. I mean, first her parents caught the plague and died. Which wasn't SO bad because she wasn't very close to them anyway, since they sent her away to a convent to be educated when she was four, and it was so far away that she hardly ever saw anyone in her family again after that.

But then all her brothers died of the plague too – which didn't bother her too much either since she hardly knew any of them.

But that meant she was the next in line to the throne.

So the nuns made Amelie pack up her stuff and go to the palace to be crowned. Which Amelie really wasn't too happy about, since she had to leave her cat, Agnès-Claire, behind.

Because cats aren't allowed at the Palais de Genovia (it's amazing how the more times change, the more they stay the same).

And when she got to the palace her dad's brother, her Uncle Francesco, whom no one in her family really liked on account of that time he kicked their dog,

Padapouf (dogs ARE allowed in the palace), was already there bossing everyone around.

And, if I remember my Genovian history correctly (and believe me, after enough torturing from Grandmere, I do), Uncle Francesco – who became Prince Francesco I after Amelie's death (actually, he's Prince Francesco the ONLY, since he was such a horrible person that no one in Genovia ever named their kid Francesco again after his death) – was disliked by everyone, not just his own family. He was the worst ruler Genovia ever knew, due to his attempting to tax the populace so heavily after the plague in order to make up for his lost tithes, that many of them starved to death.

He also had a reputation for profligacy (as his nearly thirty illegitimate children, all of whom tried to make a claim for the throne after he died, proved). In fact, during Francesco's rule, Genovia very nearly became absorbed into France, as the prince owed so much money due to his gambling debts, even losing the crown jewels in a card game with William III of England at one point (they weren't recovered until nearly a century later, when a cagey Princess Margarethe seduced them away from George III, who was rumoured to be not quite right in the head).

Anyway, thanks to Francesco basically thinking he was already prince, even though he wasn't – yet – poor Amelie didn't have anything to do. So, like any bored teen with no one to talk to – all the ladies-in-waiting were dead of the plague – she went to the palace library and started reading all the books there. A bit like Belle in *Beauty and the Beast* actually! Except the Beast was her uncle, so no chance of a love connection there.

And instead of dancing teacups and candlesticks, there were just pustule-covered chancellors and stuff.

That's as far as I've gotten. It's so boring I probably wouldn't go on.

But I want to find out what happens to the cat.

I –

I just got an email. Check it out:

Cheergrl: Hey, Mia! It's me, Lana. Hope you had fun last night doing whatever. You missed an AWESOME party. You can see photos from it at lastnightsparty.com. OMG, on the way home I thought I saw your friend Lilly making out with a ninja or something at Around the Clock. But what would she be doing with a NINJA? I definitely partied WAY too hard. So how are those Louboutains from Saks working out for you? Too bad you can't wear stilettos to school. Well, TTYL! ~*Lana*~

So Lilly's romance with one of Kenny's Muay Thai fighter friends continues! If you can call what they have together a 'romance'.

When is Lilly going to realize that she'll never find the emotional fulfilment she's looking for in a relationship that's based on pure physical attraction? I mean, what kind of Muay Thai fighter can keep up with Lilly on an intellectual basis? She's going to toss him to the kerb as soon as he opens his mouth.

It's sad really. You would the think the daughter of

two psychoanalysts would be able to recognize her own pathology for what it is.

But I guess since Lilly's not in formal therapy, like I am, she thinks she doesn't have a problem.

Ha!

Which reminds me – school tomorrow.

And I haven't done any of my make-up work.

I wonder if I can get a note from Dr Knutz? *Please excuse Mia from her homework. She is depressed. Sincerely, Arthur T. Knutz.*

Yeah. That'd go over great. Especially with Ms Martinez –

OH MY GOD. Another email from Michael just popped into my inbox.

OK, I have got to stop having a panic attack every time this happens. I mean, we're friends now. He's going to write to me. I've got to stop losing it when he does. I've got to be normal. I can't keep hyperventilating just because he's reached out to me through cyberspace.

Because I'm sure he's not writing because he's realized what an awful, terrible mistake he's made, saying he just want to be friends, and that he wants to get back together. I'm sure that's not it at all. I'm sure he's just wondering why I never replied to his last email.

Or maybe I'm on some kind of forward list of his, and this is just some update on his eternal quest for an egg sandwich in Japan or whatever.

Well. I guess I'd better click on it, or I'll never know.

Maybe I'll just wait for my heart rate to go down a little . . .

Dear Mia,

Hey, heard you had bronchitis. That sucks. Hope you're feeling better now.

Things here are still good. We're already working hard on the first stage of the robotic arm – or Charlie, as we're calling it. I'm even starting to get used to the food, though baby squid isn't really my idea of a snack.

I understand my sister's been giving you a hard time. You know how Lilly is, Mia. She'll get over it eventually. You just have to give her space.

I know you're feeling under the weather and probably swamped with homework and princess stuff, but if you get a chance I'd love to hear from you.

Michael

Oh . . . God.

After I spent about half an hour crying over this email, I deleted it without replying.

Because I mean, seriously. I *can't* be friends with him.

I just can't.

I'd rather have the plague.

Monday, September 20, French

Mia - what is that you're reading?

It's nothing, Tina. Just a journal belonging to one of my ancestresses.

Does it have a hot romance in it?????

Um . . . not really. It's actually kind of boring. Right now she's just drafting some kind of executive order based on something she read in the palace library. Not that it's going to do anybody any good. She, along with almost everybody else in the palace, dies of the plague at the end.

That doesn't sound like your kind of read at all!

Yeah, I know. I don't know what's come over me lately.

Well, a lot's been going on. Naturally, you're growing and changing with the times. Speaking of growing - is that your new uniform?

Oh, yeah, it is. Thank God it came. I thought I was going to suffocate in that old one. Although I guess it wasn't nearly as bad as the corsets they made my ancestress wear. Hey, did you hear Lilly was out this weekend with her mystery Muay Thai fighter man?

No! Who'd you hear that from?

Uh, I forget. Anyway, T, this is serious. You have to find out the 411 on this guy! Lilly could get seriously hurt.

I don't know, I'm not exactly Lilly's favourite person these days either. It's like she hates me for still hanging out with you. You might have better luck with Kenny in your chem class.

Right. I'm on it. Oh my God, did you know that in the 1600s people wore the lice they'd picked off you in lockets as a sign of affection?

Gross! I'm glad we have Claire's Boutique instead.

Seriously.

Monday, September 20, Gifted and Talented

You know, I really didn't think things could get any worse than my boyfriend dumping me and my best friend deciding I'm a cheating ho and refusing to speak to me any more. Oh, and someone starting a website about what a dork I am and how much they hate me.

Then Lana Weinberger deciding she's my new best friend.

Look. I'm not saying I can't use any more friends. Because God knows, I can.

But I'm just not sure I'm ready to have QUITE AS MANY FRIENDS as I apparently have now.

Especially since all I really want to do is get back in my bed and stay there.

Preferably forever.

But no. Clearly this is asking way, way too much.

Because today at lunch, when I went to sit down by Tina and Boris and J.P., I was astonished to find Lana and Trisha had put their trays down beside mine as well.

'Oh my God,' Lana said when she saw what I was having for lunch. 'Are you eating the corn dog? Do you have any idea how many carbs are in that? No wonder you've gone up a size. Hey, are those the new earrings you got Saturday? They look cute.'

Oh, yes. I was outed:

Outed as being a Friend of Lana's.

Well, whatever. I mean, she's not THAT bad. Sure, we've had our differences in the past.

But she does have some really great tips on how to stop biting your nails (put Sally Hansen Hard As Nails on them every night without fail before bed, and after an olive-oil cuticle rub).

Tina was staring at Lana with her mouth hanging open in astonishment, causing Trisha to say, 'Take a picture, sweetie, it'll last longer,' then remark that she liked the way Tina does her eyeliner, and asked if wearing it that way was part of her religion or what.

This caused Tina to choke on her tuna salad.

'So do any of you have Schuyler for pre-calc?' Lana wanted to know. 'Because I don't have a freaking clue what's going on in that class.'

To which Boris replied, looking pained, 'Um . . . I do.'

And then he spent the rest of the lunch period helping Lana with her homework, while Tina spent the rest of the lunch period showing Trisha how she does her eyes, and J.P. spent the rest of the lunch period smirking into his chilli (sans corn).

All I wanted to do was read my translation of Amelie's journal. But I couldn't, because I was worried about how that might look. You know, that it might appear antisocial.

And I have enough strikes against me at the moment without 'antisocial' being added to the list.

I did notice Lilly give me a very dirty look over her shoulder as she went to take her tray up to the counter.

But that might have been because I was letting Lana put mini barrettes in my hair and Lilly has a thing about personal grooming in the caff.

Monday, September 20, Chemistry

J.P. wants to know how, merely by going shopping with Lana, I became one of the In-Crowd.

I told him Lana and I didn't merely go shopping: we went bra shopping.

To which J.P. replied, 'Please tell me all about it. And I mean *all*.'

But I was too busy reading about Princess Amelie. Uncle Francesco busted into the palace library and ordered all the books there to be burned, just to be mean, I'm sure, because he happened to know Amelie really liked them, not because he seriously believed they were contributing to the spread of the disease.

As if that wasn't upsetting enough, he also threw the drafts of the executive order she'd so carefully penned and signed – and had *witnessed*, which was no joke, since it was hard to find two living people in the palace to witness the signing of a document – into the fire. Even though Amelie explained to him that whatever it was she'd drawn up had been for the good of the Genovian people! Whom she did not believe he cared about. Especially since they were dropping like flies, and yet he was still allowing foreign ships to dock in the port, which only seemed to be bringing more disease into the country . . . not to mention spreading it back to the towns the ships had come from, on their return trip.

Amelie accused her uncle of only caring about whether or not the olive oil got delivered. To Uncle Francesco, it was *always* about the olive oil. And the crown, of course.

But no! He thought burning books (and executive orders) was the answer to all their problems!

I really wanted to keep reading because things were finally getting good with poor Amelie (or bad, as the case might be).

But Kenny yelled at me that if I wasn't going to help with the experiment, I could just accept the zero I deserved.

So I'm stirring. Which would explain why my handwriting looks so bad.

Monday, September 20, 4 p.m. the Loft

Even though I am still in the depths of despair and all, I was actually kind of excited after school today because

A) No princess lessons

B) Even though I have no TV, I have something totally excellent to read.

I fully intended to take off my school uniform, put on my sweats and curl up in bed to read about my ancestress.

But my (admittedly mild) excitement was short-lived, due to walking into the loft and finding Mr G at the dining-room table with all the assignments that I missed last week.

'Sit,' he said, holding out a chair.

So I sat.

And now we're tackling all my make-up work. One class at a time.

This is so unfair.

Monday, September 20, 11 p.m., the Loft

Oh my God I am so tired. And we're not even halfway caught up with everything.

What is the POINT of piling so much work on to us? Don't they know that all they are doing is breaking our already fragile spirits? Is this really what the powers that be want? A generation of wounded, broken souls?

No wonder so many teens turn to drugs. I would too, if I weren't so tired. And I could find some.

So, it turns out Uncle Francesco didn't appreciate Amelie saying he didn't care about the people of Genovia. He told her that if *she* really cared about the people of Genovia, she'd step down and let him rule. Because she's just a girl who doesn't have any idea what she's doing.

!!!!!!!!!!!!!

But I guess Amelie had more of an idea about what she was doing than she let on, because she drew up ANOTHER executive order – this one was to close all Genovian roads and ports. No one was allowed in or out of the country. She did this because she thought it might do a little more to reduce the spread of the plague than burning all the books in the town.

Ha! Take that, Francesco, you loser!

Also, she had the best mousers in the city brought to the palace. Because she couldn't help noticing that in places where there were cats – like back at the convent, where she'd left Agnès-Claire – there'd been no outbreaks of the disease.

For a girl who lived in the 1600s and had had no formal education, Princess Amelie was pretty smart.

Oh, and she had her uncle thrown out of the castle.

Man. And I thought MY family was dysfunctional.

Tuesday, September 21, Intro to Creative Writing

My relatives turn out not to be the only ones conspiring against me. The minute I walked in to school today, Principal Gupta was waiting for me. She crooked her finger at me to follow her into her office. Lars and I exchanged panicky looks, like – *Uh-oh*! I couldn't figure out what we'd done now.

Or what *I*'d done, anyway. I was sure Principal Gupta must have found out about the time I pulled the fire alarm when there wasn't really a fire. True, that was a year ago, but maybe that's how long it had taken them to go through all the video surveillance of the hallways or something . . .

But it turned out to have nothing to do with that. Instead, she confiscated my journal.

I am writing this in my chemistry notebook right now.

Principal Gupta said, 'Mia, I understand you're going through a rough time right now. But your grades are slipping. You're a junior in high school. Soon colleges will be looking at your transcripts.'

I wanted to point out to her what she and everyone else knows perfectly well: that I am going to get into every college I apply to. Because I'm a princess. I wish it weren't true. But it is. I mean, even Lana knows it.

'I understand from Mrs Potts,' Principal Gupta went on, 'that you were even writing in your journal during physical-education class the other day. This can't go on. You can't expect to be able to slide by just because you're a minor celebrity, Mia.'

Talk about unfair! I have never tried to slide by on my celebrity, however minor!

'Consider writing in your journal during class *verboten* from this moment on,' Principal Gupta said. 'I am holding on to your journal – don't worry, I will NOT read it – until classes let out for the day. You may have it back then. And kindly do NOT bring it to school again tomorrow. Is that understood?'

What could I say? I mean . . . she's not wrong.

She's instructed all my teachers to take away any paper they catch me writing on, unless it's class-related. I am only getting away with writing this because Ms Martinez thinks it's the creative-writing assignment she just gave us, to describe a moment that touched us deeply.

You know what moment touched me deeply?

When Principal Gupta locked my journal in the school safe. It was like being gutted open with a Bic disposable pen.

Tuesday, September 21, English

Mia - where's your journal?????

I don't want to talk about it.

Oh. OK. I'm sorry!

No, I'm sorry. That was rude. It's just – Principal Gupta took it away. Because my grades are slipping.

Oh, Mia! That's terrible!

No it's not. It's my own fault. I'm not supposed to be passing notes either. All the teachers are supposed to take anything away they see me writing on that's not class-related. So look out.

We'll be careful then. Anyway, I wanted to say - that was kind of weird yesterday at lunch, huh? I didn't know you and Lana had become such good friends! When did that happen? I mean, if you don't mind me asking?

No, it's OK. I should have told you. I just felt weird about it. I know she's been really mean to you in the past, and I didn't – well, I just didn't want you to hate me.

Mia! I could never hate you! You know that!

Thanks, Tina. But you're the only one.

What are you talking about? No one could ever hate you!

Uh . . . a lot of people hate me actually. And Lilly REALLY hates me.

Oh. Well. LILLY. You know why she hates you.

Right. Your J.P. theory. Which is wrong. Anyway, I'm supposed to give this speech at the end of the week for this charity function Lana's mother's in charge of, and one thing led to another, and . . . she really isn't that bad, you know. I mean, she's BAD. But not AS BAD as we previously thought. I think. Do you know what I mean?

I think so. At least, when she says snarky things, it seems like she just doesn't know better than like she means to be hurtful.

I know. Kind of like Lindsay Lohan.

Exactly! Still. I don't think Lilly's too happy about it.

What do you mean? Did she say something about me?

Well, she doesn't speak to ME any more either, since I'm friends with you, so no, she didn't say anything to me. But I saw her giving you dirty looks across the caff.

Oh yeah. I saw those too. I —

I will not pass notes in class.
I will not pass notes in class.
I will not pass notes in class.
I will not pass notes in class.
I will not pass notes in class.
I will not pass notes in class.
I will not pass notes in class.
I will not pass notes in class.
I will not pass notes in class.
I will not pass notes in class.
I will not pass notes in class.
I will not pass notes in class.
I will not pass notes in class.
I will not pass notes in class.
I will not pass notes in class.
I will not pass notes in class.
I will not pass notes in class.
I will not pass notes in class.
I will not pass notes in class.
I will not pass notes in class.
I will not pass notes in class.
I will not pass notes in class.

Tuesday, September 21, Lunch

I apologized NON-STOP to Tina for getting her into trouble in English. Thank GOD our note didn't get read out loud. That is the only good thing.

Tina says not to worry about it, that it's nothing.

But it's NOT nothing. I can't believe I am dragging my friends down with me. It's just WRONG and I've got to STOP.

Anyway, they can't stop me from writing at LUNCH. Even if I have to do it in my chemistry notebook.

Though it's very hard to write with Lana jostling me every minute and going, 'Wait, so Gupta says you need to work harder if you want to get into college? Oh my God, that is so easily rectified. Just join the Spirit Squad. Seriously, we don't even DO anything, except have bake sales like every five weeks. Oooh, or I know! You could join *Hola* – the Spanish club. We just sit around and watch movies in Spanish. Like that one where the hot guys fight to the death with the hams. Well, we didn't really watch that one in class because it was too sexy, so Trisha and I watched it at home for extra credit. Oh, or the dance committee! We're working on the Non-Denominational Winter Dance right now! It's going to be so rockin' this year, we're trying to get an actual band instead of a DJ for a change? Or there's peer tutoring. Oh my God, I'm tutoring the cutest little second-grader right now. I totally taught her to stay within the lines with her eyeshadow.'

I was just like, 'Um. You know, I already have a lot going on, with the princess stuff. And the school paper.'

'Right,' Lana said. 'Hey, what do you think of glitter gel? You know, for my nails? Too much?'

When did this become my life?

Oh, right, I remember. The day my ex-boyfriend dumped me and I lost the will to live.

Tuesday, September 21, Gifted and Talented

OK, they can't keep me from writing in here, because

A) No one knows what I'm supposed to be doing in this stupid class anyway, given the fact that I am neither gifted nor talented, and

B) Mrs Hill isn't even here. There must be an auction on eBay she's trying to win or something, because she's in the Teachers' Lounge.

Anyway, the strangest thing just happened. After lunch I went to the Girls' Room, and while I was washing my hands Lilly came out of one of the stalls and started washing HER hands.

She was totally ignoring me, like I didn't even exist. Just gazing at herself in the mirror.

I don't know what came over me. Suddenly, I just couldn't take it any more. I turned off the water in my sink and grabbed some paper towels and ALMOST went, while I was drying my hands, 'You know what, Lilly? You can ignore me all you want, but it doesn't change the fact that you're wrong. I DID NOT cause your break-up with J.P., and I am NOT going out with him. We're JUST friends. I can't believe that after all these years of friendship, you'd even THINK that of me. And besides, you know I love your brother. I mean, despite the fact that we're just friends now too.'

But I didn't.

I didn't say a word.

Because why should I? Why should I make the first move, when *I* didn't do anything wrong? She's the one giving *me* the cold shoulder, when *I'm* the one in great personal pain. I mean, has it ever occurred to her that I could really use a friend right now? Has it ever occurred to her that now isn't the best time to be giving me the silent treatment?

But it seems like whenever I'm going through a time of personal crisis – when I found out I was a princess; when her brother dumped me – Lilly turns her back on me.

Lilly must have known I was thinking about saying something to her though, because she gave me the dirtiest look. Then she rinsed off her hands, turned off the taps, got some paper towels of her own, tossed them into the trash – the same way she seems to have tossed our friendship into the trash – and walked out without a word.

I almost ran after her. I really did. I almost ran after her and told her that, whatever it was I did, I'm sorry, and that I know I'm a freak, but I'm trying to get help. I almost went, 'Look, I'm in therapy. Are you happy now? You've driven me into therapy!'

But, number one, I know that's not true. I'm not in therapy because of Lilly or Michael or anyone really, except the Giant Hole.

And number two – well, I still have *some* pride left. I mean, I wasn't about to give her the satisfaction.

Besides, what if she told Michael or something? Then he'd think I was so torn up about our breaking up that I'm suicidal.

Which I'm *not*.

I'm just sad. Dr K even said so.

I'm just sad.

So, anyway. I let her walk out. And I never said a word.

And now I'm sitting here in G and T, watching her chat on her phone with Perin about their cell-tower initiative.

You know what? I'm not even sure I *want* to be her friend any more. I mean, to be honest, Lana Weinberger is actually a BETTER friend than Lilly ever was. At least with Lana you know where you stand. It's true Lana's completely self-absorbed and shallow.

But at least she doesn't try to pretend she's otherwise. Unlike some people I could mention.

God, I am going to have SO MUCH to talk about with Dr K on Friday.

Tuesday, September 21, 4 p.m., Chanel

Principal Gupta was all, 'Mia. Let's talk,' in a super-meaningful way when I went to snag my journal back from her.

So I had to sit down and listen to her yammer on about what a bright girl I am, with so much to offer – it's such a shame I quit student council and that I'm not taking part in more extra-curricular activities this year. Colleges, she said, look at other things besides grades and teacher recommendations, you know. They want to see that applicants to their schools also have interests outside academics.

Lana was so right about *Hola.*

'I'm on the school paper,' I offered lamely.

'Mia,' Principal Gupta said. 'You haven't gone to one newspaper meeting all semester.'

I'd been hoping she hadn't noticed that.

'Well,' I said. 'It's been kind of a bad semester.'

'I know,' Principal Gupta said. Behind her glasses, her eyes were kind. For once. 'Clearly, you've been through a lot lately. But you can't just shut down because of a boy, Mia.'

I blinked at her in horror. I mean, even if that might be true, I can't believe she'd *say* that.

'I'm *n-not,*' I stammered. 'This has nothing to do with Michael. I mean, yeah, I'm sad we broke up. But – it's just . . . it's a lot more than that.'

'What really disturbs me,' Principal Gupta said, 'is that you seem to have given up your old friends as well. I've noticed that you're no longer sitting with Lilly Moscovitz at lunch.'

'*She*'s not sitting with me,' I said indignantly. 'I'm not the one who—'

'And I've noticed you've been spending time instead with Lana Weinberger.' Principal Gupta's mouth got all small, the way my mom's does when she's mad. 'While I must say I'm grateful you and Lana aren't at each other's throats any more, I can't help but wonder if she's someone with whom you really have all that much in common –'

Now that I have boobs, she is. She knows EVERY-THING about nipple coverage.

And how to show them off as well, when it's appropriate to do that.

'I really appreciate your worrying about me, Dr Gupta,' I said. 'But you have to remember something . . .'

She looked at me expectantly. 'Yes?'

'I'm a princess,' I said. 'I'm going to get into every college I apply to, because colleges want to brag that they have a girl who's going to rule a country some day in their incoming freshman class. So it doesn't really matter if I join the Spanish club or the Spirit Squad or whatever. But –' I waved my journal at her – 'thanks for caring.'

No sooner had I stepped out of Dr G's office than my cellphone rang and I looked down to find Grandmere was calling me.

Great. Because my day could not, evidently, get any better.

'Amelia,' she sang when I picked up. 'What's keeping you? I'm WAITING.'

'Grandmere? What do you mean? We don't princess lessons this week.'

'I know that,' Grandmere said. 'I'm outside the school in the limo. Today we're going to Chanel to find something for you to wear to the gala on Friday. Remember?'

No, I did not remember. But what choice did I have? None.

So here I am at Chanel.

The staff is very excited about my new measurements. Mainly because they no longer have to take the chest darts in on the bodice of any dresses Grandmere chooses for me.

The suit she's picked out for the gala is pretty nice actually. *And* she's finally letting me wear black.

'Your first Chanel suit,' she keeps murmuring with a sigh. 'Where did the time go? It seems like just yesterday you were a scabby-kneed fourteen-year-old, who came to me not even knowing how to use a fish knife! Now look at you! BREASTS!'

Whatever. I never had scabs on my knees.

Then Grandmere handed me the speech she'd had en for me. For the gala. I guess she'd given up idea of letting me write my own speech. She'd ead and hired a former presidential speech- come up with a twenty-minute soliloquy on drainage. The speech-writer she got is very famous one, who wrote some script nd points of light.

e used to write for *Star Trek: The Next* thing.

memorize my speech, Grandmere more 'spontaneous'.

read while they're fitting me for

176

Only I'm not reading my speech. Because Grand-mere's off trying to find her own dress for the gala. Since she's been invited to attend as my 'chaperone'. I know she's hoping we'll BOTH get invites to pledge the Domina Reis.

Which might not be so bad actually. Then I can tell Principal Gupta I have an extra-curricular to put on my college apps after all. That will make her happy.

Anyway, Princess Amelie's uncle didn't stay far from the palace for long after she threw him out. That's because there were no guards left to keep him away, since they all had the plague too. He came back and kept telling Amelie how much money she was losing by not allowing the ships importing Genovian olive oil to leave the ports. Also by not demanding that the Genovian people continue to tithe to her, even though they had no money, since they all had the plague and couldn't work.

But Uncle Francesco didn't care. He kept saying she didn't know what she was doing because she was Just A Girl, and how she was going to bankrupt the Renaldo royal family and go down in history as the worst Genovian ruler of all time.

How ironic that, in the end, HE was the one who earned this distinction.

Anyway, Amelie told her uncle to back off. She knew she was saving lives. Fewer new cases of the disease were being reported because of her initiatives.

Too late for her though. Because she'd noticed her first pustule.

She decided not to tell her uncle. Because Amelie knew when she went, he'd get what he wanted: the throne, which was all he cared about. He didn't care if there were no people left over whom to rule. He just wanted her money. And her crown.

Which she wasn't about to relinquish just then. Because there was one more thing she had to do.

Too bad Grandmere's back and WON'T STOP TALKING SO I CAN FIND OUT WHAT IT WAS!

Wednesday, September 22, 1 a.m., the Loft

Oh my God! That was so sad! Princess Amelie totally died!

I mean, I knew she was sick.

And, obviously, I knew she was going to die.

But it was just so . . . traumatic! She was completely alone! There was no one even to hand her a tissue in the end because everyone else was dead (except her uncle, but he stayed away because he didn't want to catch what she had).

Plus, there were no such things as tissues back then.

That is just so . . . wrong.

Not about the tissues. About being alone.

I can't stop crying now. Which is, you know, great. Since I have to get up and go to school tomorrow. For some reason. And it's not like I haven't exactly been depressed anyway. This is just, you know. Another shove further down that hole.

I don't even know why I bother to go on. I mean, look at the facts:

We're born.

We live for a little bit of time.

And then we die, our uncle assumes the throne, burns all our stuff and does everything he possibly can to illegitimize the twelve days we spent ruling by basically being the suckiest prince of all time.

At least Amelie managed to save her journal, which – she wrote, on the last few pages – she intended to send back to the convent where she'd been so comparatively happy, for safe keeping, along with her little portrait. The nuns, she said, would 'know what to do'.

There's something else she managed to save from

burning too – aside from Agnès-Claire, whom I have to imagine died happy and full of mice at the abbey where her mistress's belongings obviously eventually showed up, only to be returned to the Genovian palace by the dutiful nuns, according to Amelie's wishes, and then to Parliament, who . . .

. . . ignored it.

I can only assume they ignored it because they all figured what could a sixteen-year-old girl have to say?

Plus, her uncle wasn't exactly making life easy for them, what with his goal to spend every last penny in Genovia's treasury. So it wasn't like they had time to go home and read some dead princess's diary.

Anyway, that other thing Amelie managed to save was one last copy of the thing she had drawn up and signed by those witnesses – whatever it was. She says she hid the parchment 'somewhere close to my heart, where some future princess will find it and do what is right'.

Except, of course, if you're dying of the plague, it's really not a good idea to hide anything close to your heart.

Because your corpse is just going to get burned to a cinder by your uncle in a fiery funeral pyre.

Wednesday, September 22, Gifted and Talented

Lana just dropped a small weapon of mass destruction on the lunch table. Just dropped it, then shrugged, like it was nothing. But that, I'm learning, is her way.

'So how long has *that* been going on?' she wanted to know, waggling her fingers at the lunch table, where Lilly was sitting with Kenny Showalter, et al.

I glanced over to where she was pointing. 'Oh. Well, Lilly isn't speaking to me for a number of reasons. First, and probably foremost, she blames me for J.P. dumping her—'

'Hey!' J.P. protested. 'I didn't dump her! I told her I thought it would be better if we were just friends.'

'Yeah. There's a lot of that going around. Secondly,' I informed Lana, 'Lilly's upset because I refused to run for student-council president. Even though I never wanted to be student-council president in the first place – she did. Thirdly, she—'

'I don't mean how long have you two been fighting,' Lana said, rolling her eyes. 'I know that. I mean, how long have she and the Beanpole been banging.'

Sometimes it's quite difficult to understand what Lana is saying, because she uses a type of slang with which no one else at our lunch table (aside from Trisha Hayes and Shameeka, who has also come back to the fold) is familiar.

'Beanpole?' I echoed.

'Banging?' Tina added.

Lana rolled her eyes again and said, 'How long has Lilly Moscovitz been sleeping with Mr Rocket Science?'

I dropped my beef and cheese taquito.

'WHAT?' I cried. 'Lilly and *Kenny*?'

But Lana just blinked her super-long volume-enhanced mascaraed lashes and went, 'Duh. I told you I saw them sucking face at Around the Clock this past weekend.'

'You said you saw Lilly and a NINJA making out,' I said. 'Not KENNY. Kenny Showalter is not a ninja.'

'No,' Lana said as she chewed her tuna-avocado roll – which she has specially delivered every day for lunch since the caff doesn't do sushi – 'it was definitely that guy over there.'

'Totally,' Trisha said. 'I'd recognize that bulbous Adam's apple anywhere. It was bobbing all over the place.'

Tina and I looked at one another in shock. Then Tina swung an accusing glare at her boyfriend.

'Boris,' she said. 'Was the guy Lilly was making out with in her kitchen KENNY?'

Boris looked uncomfortable. 'It was hard to tell,' he said. 'His back was to me. And all those Muay Thai fighters looked the same with their shirts off.'

'Oh my God!' Tina cried. 'It *was* Kenny! Boris! You got Mia all upset for nothing, thinking Lilly was hooking up with a random, strange Muay Thai fighter in her despair over J.P. dumping her, when really it was Kenny all along!'

'I didn't dump her!' J.P. insisted.

But Boris just looked bored. 'Who cares?' he wanted to know. 'When are things going to go back to *normal* round here?'

On the word *normal*, he looked over at Lana and Trisha.

No one, of course, noticed. Except for J.P., who smiled at me. J.P. really *does* have a nice smile.

Not that that has anything to do with any of this.

Anyway, at first I was like, 'But Lilly could so easily break Kenny's neck with her thighs, like Daryl Hannah in *Blade Runner*.'

But then I remembered how Kenny's been bulking up with all that Muay Thai fighting.

So. I'm happy for her. I really am. I mean, if she's happy, I'm happy.

But still. KENNY SHOWALTER????????

Wednesday, September 22, Chemistry

I don't care about the ban on my writing in class: I HAVE to get this down.

I couldn't stand it any more. I HAD to ask Kenny what was going on with him and Lilly.

So I just went, 'Kenny. Is it true about you and Lilly going out? Because if so I want you to know I think you guys make a really nice couple.' (Lie. But since when do I ever tell the truth?)

Anyway, Kenny totally didn't seem to appreciate my kind remarks. He went, 'Mia! Do you mind? I'm in the acid-neutralization phase!'

So then I was like, 'Fine. Sorry I said anything,' and went back to my stool to write this.

And then a second ago J.P. sat down next to me and was like, 'So, am I in the clear now?'

And I was like, 'In the clear for what?'

And he was like, 'Breaking Lilly's heart. Now that she's learned to love again, as Tina would put it.'

So I laughed and said, 'J.P., whatever, I never blamed you for what happened between you and Lilly. You can't help it if you didn't feel the same way about her that she felt about you.'

Although he could probably have helped by not leading her on for so long. But I didn't add that part out loud.

'I'm glad you feel that way, Mia,' J.P. said. 'Because there's something I've been meaning to tell you for a long time now and, every time I start to, something seems to happen to interrupt me, so I'm just going to say it now, even though this might not be the ideal mo—

Wednesday, September 22, East 75th Street, AEHS Evacuation Rendezvous Point

Oh my God.
   Oh my God.
   J.P. is in love with me.
   And we blew up the school.

Wednesday, September 22, Lenox Hill Hospital Emergency Room

To tell you the truth, I didn't know which to write first back then.

I mean, I don't know which is more upsetting – that it turns out J.P. has fallen in love with me, or that we all nearly died from Kenny's experiment, in which he was trying to recreate – unbeknownst to the rest of us – a substance formerly used as filler in hand grenades during the Second World War, with a very high deflagration point – which means, in English, that it's very unstable and BLOWS UP A LOT.

And we weren't even supposed to be making it! Mr Hipskin didn't realize that's what we were doing because Kenny told him we were making nitrocellulose, which is flash paper similar to what's used in film.

Not nitrostarch, which is an EXPLOSIVE!

The emergency-room nurse keeps assuring me that Kenny's eyebrows will grow back some day.

I was much luckier. I'm here in the ER under protest – there's nothing actually wrong with me. They just sent me here to avoid a lawsuit, I'm sure. I mean, I only had the wind knocked out of me. That's because just before deflagration occurred, when Kenny yelled, 'Everybody get down!' J.P. threw me off my stool and flattened his body over mine, so all the flaming debris landed on him and not me.

Which, I might add, was right after he'd said, 'Because there's something I've been meaning to tell you for a long time now and, every time I start to, something seems to happen to interrupt me, so I'm just going to say it now, even though this might not be the ideal moment. And I know you're going to freak out now, because that's what you do. So put down your pen and take a deep breath.'

This is when his blue eyes locked on to my grey ones and he said, super intently and without looking away, 'Mia, I'm in love with you. I know up until now we've just been friends – good friends – but I want more than that. And I think you do too.'

It was right then that Kenny yelled to get down. And that J.P. threw himself at me.

Fortunately for J.P., Lars was ON IT with the fire extinguisher – I guess to make up for not being the one to throw himself over me, which is, after all, his job, and not J.P.'s – and put out the flames that erupted on the back of J.P.'s sweater. He didn't even get burned, because our school uniforms are made of so many unnatural fibres, most of which are flame retardant.

So no flames actually ever touched J.P.'s skin. Just his V-neck.

All of us had to flee a cloud of billowing nitrogen-dioxide vapour though. And not just in our chem class either. The whole school.

Good thing it wasn't freezing outside (some kind of cold front has come down from Canada, making the city unseasonably cool for September), and none of us had our coats or anything. Not.

One of the nurses just came in and said the whole thing was on Channel One – a live shot from a helicopter of everyone standing outside Albert Einstein High, shivering, with the fire trucks and ambulances all flashing their lights and everything.

Only three people were actually taken to the hospital though: J.P., Kenny and me.

Principal Gupta caught me just before they closed the ambulance doors. She was all, 'Mia, I want to give you my sincerest assurances that I intend to get to the bottom of this matter. Mr Showalter will *not* go unpunished . . .'

I pointed out that having no eyebrows is punishment enough, if you ask me. But Dr Gupta had already moved on to J.P.'s ambulance, to repeat the same thing.

Which was smart of her because I hear J.P.'s dad is TOTALLY litigious.

It's funny that no one has said anything about the fact that J.P. and I were Kenny's lab partners, and we certainly never tried to stop him from blowing up the school. Except that both of us are so bad at chemistry we didn't know that's what he was trying to do.

Of course, Kenny swears destroying the chem lab was never his goal. He only, he claims, wanted to figure out how a synthesis of nitrostarch could be performed in a lab setting. Also, that he doesn't know how it got so out of control. He says it was perfectly stable just seconds before . . . and then WHAMMO.

To tell the truth, I'm kind of glad Kenny's experiment conflagrated. Because it kept me from having to figure out how to respond to J.P.'s totally shocking announcement that he's in love with me.

Which, frankly, I find really hard to believe. Considering the fact that just two weeks ago, he and Lilly were totally an item.

And, OK, it wasn't as if they didn't have problems. I mean, Lilly was pretty upset that J.P. never said, *Me too* to her when she told him that she loved him.

188

But he *explained* that. He explained that he never felt that way about her, and that's why he broke up with her, because he realized it wasn't fair to her. He did the right thing . . . even if she hates him for it now.

And me, too, for still being friendly with him.

But that doesn't mean – despite Tina's insane theory about J.P. having always been in love with me and not Lilly from the beginning – that he was really in love with *me* that whole time. In fact, J.P. explained – as Lars was putting out the flames on his back – that his feelings for me had been coming on gradually, and he'd only decided to mention it because he couldn't stand seeing me so sad about Michael.

'J.P.,' I'd gasped. It was hard to talk with all the breath knocked out of me. Also because of the toxic fumes. 'We'll discuss this later, OK?'

'But I really need to tell you now,' J.P. insisted.

'PRINCESS, RUN!' Lars was yelling. Because by then the cloud of noxious fumes was descending upon us.

Fortunately, since J.P. and I were taken away in separate ambulances, I had a chance to process this – sort of – and figure out what I'm going to do about it.

Which I'm pretty sure is nothing.

And yes, I know Dr Knutz wouldn't approve. He'd want me to do whatever scared me most.

Which, in this case, would be to date J.P.

But I can't! I'm not ready! I'm barely broken up with my last long-term boyfriend – with whom I am still hopelessly in love! I can't jump into another romantic relationship this soon!

Besides, I don't feel that way about J.P. When I smell him, my oxytocin levels don't rise. When I sniffed him

189

the other night when he hugged me, I felt . . . nothing. All I smelt was dry-cleaning fluid.

Which is so not what I smell when Michael holds me, which is . . . well, OK, it's just like soap and stuff.

But it's not just ANY soap smell. It's the special way Michael's skin – and Michael's skin alone – smells when he uses Dove unscented moisturizing beauty bar. That, and the detergent he uses on his shirts, combined with that particular Michael smell, just makes . . .

. . . well, the best smell in the world.

I know it doesn't make sense. But I'm just not sure I'm ready to move on from unscented Dove/detergent/Michael to . . . dry-cleaning fluid.

And what about HIM? What about J.P.? I mean, how much of this 'love' thing is just a reaction to the discovery that Lilly has rebounded already with someone new? The timing is a little suspicious. I mean, we find out at lunch that Lilly and Kenny are an item and, all of a sudden, J.P. loves me? Come on!

And, OK, he says he's been trying to tell me for a while . . . but I'm positive that can't be true. Because up until very recently, I've been taken!

And J.P. knows I haven't gotten over Michael yet. He has to know that the chances are I will NEVER get over Michael. At least, not for a long, long time. He wouldn't be silly enough to fall in love with me knowing I could never return his feelings in that way . . .

Before senior year or so, anyway.

And, all right, J.P. does currently have a bit of a Dr McDreamy quality about him, since the hospital has given him scrubs to change into because his sweater melted and his shirt is all scorched. So he looks pretty cute.

And he did save my life and all . . .

ACK! I am in no condition to deal with this right now! I just want to go home and get into my bed and try to sort out how I feel about all this!

Not the almost getting blown up part. *That* part I can deal with. I mean, at this point, getting almost blown up is NOTHING compared to the humiliations I go through on an almost daily basis.

But the J.P. loving me part? It's too weird! What could make him think I'd ever feel that way about him? Because I don't!

At least, I think I don't. I mean, I like him a lot. He's one of my best friends – especially now that Lilly has dropped me.

But he's not Michael.

He's not Michael.

He's not Michael.

Oh, here comes the doctor . . .

Wednesday, September 22, 11 p.m. the Loft

I'm home . . .

I don't even care that I don't have a TV any more. It's just so nice to be in my own bed, where no nitrostarches can explode, and no boys can announce their love for me.

You know, you would think, after everything that happened today, they'd finally let me move to Genovia and be palace-schooled now. For my own *physical and emotional safety*.

But no. Mr G just informed me that Albert Einstein is going to be cleaned up and fully functional tomorrow – including the chem lab, which has been thoroughly fumigated, *and* they've already replaced the glass that was blown out of the windows (stupid emergency glaziers), and that I'm going to be there, just like everybody else.

Well, except for Kenny, who's suspended for knowingly creating a secondary explosive in the lab. When I protested that if they were suspending Kenny they ought to suspend me and J.P. as well, since we're his lab partners, Mr G just looked at me and went, 'Mia. I've been trying to get you caught up in all your classes this week, remember? Believe me, I know you and J.P. have no clue what you're doing in that class.'

Which, you know. Harsh. But true, I guess.

So it looks like Kenny's going to get his fifteen minutes of fame now, as opposed to after he starts working for Michael's robotic-surgical-arm company, as he once asked me if I thought he could. What happened today at school is ALL OVER the news and Internet. Reporters are calling Kenny 'Beaker' after that mad-scientist Muppet character (which is mean, since Kenny really does have quite a lot of upper-arm definition these days. And his mouth isn't a gaping flap. Not as much as it used to be anyway), and keep showing a picture of him being led off to the ambulance, with his hair in all these crazy puffs on the top of his head.

That, coupled with his singed lab coat and the whole no-eyebrow thing, lent him a not dissimilar appearance to a certain dowager princess – not Muppet – that I know.

The thing's been aired so many times by now, I'm SURE Michael must have heard about it. Every single article describes J.P. as this huge hero for throwing his body over mine and protecting me from the flames.

And every single article calls him 'Princess Mia's new boyfriend'.

Yeah. Nice.

I was almost afraid to check my email. But I needn't have worried. Michael didn't write.

Tina IM'd the minute she saw I was online though.

```
Iluvromance: Oh my God, Mia!!!! Have you seen
             the news????
>
FtLouie:     Seen it? I thought I WAS the
             news.
>
Iluvromance: I can't believe this! Poor
             Kenny! They suspended him!
>
FtLouie:     Well, he DID blow up the chem
             lab.
>
```

Iluvromance: I know! But he didn't mean to. You know that. I really hope this won't go down on his permanent record. It could totally affect his chances of getting into college!

>

FtLouie: I'm sure Kenny will be just fine, Tina. I mean, don't forget, he DID manage to make a bomb from scratch. I wouldn't be surprised if he doesn't get hired straight out of high school by the NSA.

>

Iluvromance: What's the NSA?

>

FtLouie: It's - never mind. Listen, did you hear what happened right BEFORE the nitrostarch deflagrated?

>

Iluvromance: You mean the part where J.P. covered your body with his in order to protect you from the raging wall of fire???? Yes!!! It's so romantic!!!!

>

FtLouie: Uh, there was no raging wall of fire. But I mean before THAT even. Tina - HE TOLD ME HE LOVES ME.

>

Iluvromance: EEEEEEEEEEEEEEEEEEEEEEEEEEEEEEE
EEEEEEEEEEEEEEEEEEEEEEEEEEEEEEE

```
                    EEEEEEEEEEEEEEEEEEEEEEEEEEEEEEEE
                    EEEEEEEEEEEEEEEEEEEEEEEEEEEEEEEE
                    EEEEEEEEEEEE.
>
FtLouie:      I know. I thought you'd say
              that.
>
Iluvromance:  I TOLD YOU!!!!!! I TOLD YOU HE
              LOVES YOU!!!! I KNEW IT!!!! OH
              MY GOD, YOU GUYS MAKE THE CUTEST
              COUPLE!!!!!! BECAUSE YOU'RE BOTH
              SO TALL AND BLOND AND BLUE-
              EYED!!!!
>
FtLouie:      My eyes are grey.
>
Iluvromance:  WHATEVER!!!! OK, tell me every-
              thing. How did he say it? What
              did you say? How did you feel?
              Have you kissed yet? Where are
              you going on your first date? Or
              - wait. Was going to Beauty and
              the Beast your first date? Did he
              tell you WHEN he knew he loved
              you? It was before he dumped
              Lilly, right? I KNEW that's why
              he ditched her. And now it
              totally makes sense why she's so
              mad at you.
```

Oh God!

```
FtLouie:      Of COURSE he didn't know he
```

liked me when he was with Lilly! Do you think I'd even entertain the idea of going out with him if I knew he always liked me and was just using Lilly for - whatever? I mean, what kind of friend would I be if I did that???

>

Iluvromance: Oh. So you mean . . . he DIDN'T always love you from the moment you first spoke to him in the caff last year? And that whole thing with Lilly WASN'T just because you were taken, and dating her was a convenient way for J.P. to stay close to you?

>

FtLouie: NO! Oh my God, Tina, are you sure you didn't inhale any of those fumes that got released this afternoon?

>

Iluvromance: Pretty sure. Wahim did a good job of hustling me out of there. Well, that IS what Dad pays him for. So, if J.P. DIDN'T love you from the moment you first spoke to him in the caff last year, how long DID he say he *has* loved you?

>

FtLouie: He said it's been coming on fairly slowly recently, and that he kept trying to tell me, but we

196

```
                    kept  getting  interrupted.  But
                    that,  even  though  he  knew  it  was
                    going  to  freak  me  out,  he  wanted
                    me  to  know.  And  then  the  chem  lab
                    exploded.
>
Iluvromance: OH  MY  GOD!!!!
>
FtLouie:            I  know.  It  was  kind  of  scary
                    actually.  At  first  I  thought  the
                    boiler  room  had  finally  exploded.
                    You  know  how  they're  always  say-
                    ing  it's  about  to  go  .  .  .
>
Iluvromance: I  DON'T  MEAN  THAT!!!  I  MEAN  -
                    Mia,  I  ALWAYS  said  that  all  J.P.
                    needed  was  the  right  woman  to
                    unlock  his  heart  -  which  up
                    until  now  he  has  kept  in  a  cold,
                    hard  shell  for  his  own  emotional
                    protection  -  and  he  will  be  like
                    an  unstoppable  volcano  of  pas-
                    sion!!!
>
FtLouie:            Yeah.  So?
>
Iluvromance: SO   HE'S   FOUND   HER!!!   AND
                    THAT'S   WHY   THE   CHEM
                    LAB   EXPLODED!!!!
```

Seriously. Sometimes I wonder how Tina got put in so many AP classes. Not to be mean or anything.

But still.

```
FtLouie:        Tina.  The   chem   lab   exploded
                because  Kenny  was  synthesizing
                nitrostarch  and  obviously  did
                something wrong -

>

Iluvromance: He   did   something   wrong,   all
                right.  What  he  did  wrong  was
                mix   such   a   volatile   chemical
                compound    within    such    close
                proximity of J.P. while J.P. was
                admitting  his  true  feelings  for
                you,  the  woman  who  has  unlocked
                his heart at last!!!!!!!
```

Oh, man. I wish I had my TV back. I really could use a nice quiet rerun of *Judging Amy* or *Joan of Arcadia* right now to soothe my nerves.

```
FtLouie:        Tina.  Come  on.  J.P.'s  passion
                for me did not cause the explo-
                sion in the chem lab today.

>

Iluvromance: Oh,  all  right,  fine.  Be  that  way
                - a  total  unromantic  about  it!
                But  you  have  to  admit,  it  IS
                awfully coincidental. So anyway.
                What did you say?

>

FtLouie:        When J.P. landed on me? I said,
                'Get  off,  you're  squishing  me
                and I can't breathe.'

>
```

198

Iluvromance: No! I mean, when he told you about his true feelings for you!

>

FtLouie: Oh. I didn't say anything really. I didn't have a chance. The chem lab exploded.

>

Iluvromance: Right. But then later?

>

FtLouie: Well, then we were in the ambulances. And then in the ER. And then J.P.'s parents came and got him. And that was it.

>

Iluvromance: THAT WAS IT??? But what did you say about his loving you? Did you say you love him too?

>

FtLouie: Of course not, Tina! I love Michael!

>

Iluvromance: Well, of course you love Michael. But, Mia, no offence – you and Michael are broken up. You can't just go on loving him forever. Well, I mean, you CAN, of course, like Ross went on loving Rachel forever on *Friends*, but . . . what about the senior prom?

>

FtLouie: What ABOUT the senior prom?

>

```
Iluvromance: Well, Mia, you need SOMEONE to
             go to the senior prom with! You
             can't not go! You could go with
             other girls, I guess, like Perin
             and Ling Su are saying they're
             going to . . . but don't you
             remember our promise? That we'd
             lose our virginity on the night
             of our senior prom?
```

I couldn't believe she was bringing this up. NOW.

```
FtLouie:     Yes, but, Tina, that was before
             the love of my life walked out of
             it.
>
Iluvromance: Oh! I know! And I'm so sorry
             things didn't work out with you
             and Michael. But, Mia, you will
             learn to love again. And J.P.
             looks really good in a tux.
             Don't listen to what the haters
             are saying.
```

What is she TALKING about? This isn't the Tina I
know, my staunchest, most stalwart supporter! The
Tina I know would never tell me I'll learn to love again.
The Tina I know would tell me to stay strong, that
Michael would be coming to his senses soon and riding
back to me on a milk-white charger, possibly in armour,
bearing a corsage of one hundred per cent zirconium
from Kay Jewelers . . .

Or not. Because this is so something Michael would never, ever do.

And even Tina – starry-eyed, romantic Tina – knows it.

I should probably admit it to myself by now.

FtLouie: Michael's never coming back, is
              he, Tina?
>
Iluvromance: Oh, Mia! Of course he *might* come
              back! The question is . . . if
              he does, will you still even
              want him? Or will you have moved
              on . . . possibly to someone
              better?

My eyes filled with tears.

FtLouie: There is no one better, Tina.
              You know that.
>
Iluvromance: There might be! You don't know!
>
FtLouie: And anyway, what's the point in
              having this conversation. He'll
              never take me back. Not after
              how stupid I was.
>
Iluvromance: He could! You never know! I TOLD
              you, don't listen to the haters!
>
FtLouie: Haters? What haters? Why do you
              keep saying that?

\>

Iluvromance: Oh – Mia, I don't care. They told
me not to tell you, but I HAVE
to. I know you're depressed, but
you have a right to know, you
know?

\>

FtLouie: About WHAT? WHAT ARE YOU TALKING
ABOUT?

\>

Iluvromance: ihatemiathermopolis.com.

\>

FtLouie: Oh. That.

\>

Iluvromance: YOU'VE BEEN THERE???? YOU KNOW
ABOUT IT????

\>

FtLouie: Sure.

\>

Iluvromance: THEN WHY DON'T YOU GET YOUR DAD
TO GET IT SHUT DOWN?????

\>

FtLouie: Tina, my dad may be a prince, but
he doesn't have control over the
Internet.

\>

Iluvromance: But   he   could   complain   to
Principal Gupta!

\>

FtLouie: Principal Gupta? Why HER? What
does SHE have to do with it?

\>

Iluvromance: Well, since the site is so obvi-

```
            ously    run    by    someone    at
            AEHS . . .
>
FtLouie:     WHAT????
```

Even though it was kind of hard to see, what with my tears and all, I clicked over to ihatemiathermopolis.com. So much had been going on in my life, I hadn't had a chance to go there in a while.

I immediately saw that neglecting the site had been a mistake. Because there had been updates since my last visit. A LOT of updates.

Whoever owned the site had been keeping a close eye on my every move. And I mean my *every* move. The day I got a drink out of the second floor water fountain at AEHS and the spray hit me in the face instead of my mouth? Recorded with glee. The time I tripped over my new shoes and dropped all my books outside the chem lab? Noted. The time I spilt soy sauce all down the front of my school uniform in the caff? There was actually a photo . . . a bad one, obviously taken with a cellphone camera.

But it was there.

And whoever had founded the site hadn't stopped there. There was loads of advice as to how I could improve my looks so as not to appear so physically repulsive. For instance, according to ihatemia-thermopolis.com, I needed to grow my hair out (well, obviously), and stop wearing my platform Mary Janes to school, because I'm 'towering over everyone like some kind of supermodel. Or so she obviously THINKS she appears. Too bad no one's told her she looks more like a superspastic'.

Nice.

That's when the tears in my eyes spilt over. Suddenly sobs were racking my body.

```
FtLouie:      Tina. I'm sorry. I have to go.
>
Iluvromance:  Mia? Are you all right? You're
              not taking this idiotic stuff
              SERIOUSLY, are you?
>
FtLouie:      No, of course not! I just have to
              go. I'll call you later.
>
Iluvromance:  Mia! I'm so sorry - but I thought
              you should know! Your dad should
              really call the school.
>
FtLouie:      I'm glad you told me. Really.
              Goodnight, Tina.
>
Iluvromance:  Goodnight -
```

Thursday, September 23, 12 a.m. the Loft

I just cried for like half an hour – in my bathroom, with the door shut and the water running, so everyone would think I was just showering, and not bother me to ask what was wrong. I think I cried harder just now than I ever have in my whole life. Fat Louie's fur is SOAKED from all the tears that dropped into it while he curled up in my lap.

Well, OK. He wasn't really curled up in my lap. I was clutching him there, and he was trying to get away, wailing piteously for help.

But whatever! If a girl can't have her cat to comfort her in her time of direst need, what good is even HAVING a cat???

It just . . . it so blows, you know? I don't WANT to be that girl. The crying, emo girl. Next thing you know, I'll start wearing skinny jeans and too much black eyeliner and nail polish and read vampire romance novels.

God. I just . . . when am I going to start feeling BETTER? When am I going to get out of this hole Dr Knutz PROMISED me he'd help me out of?

And it's so lame, because I know how LUCKY I am. I mean, I don't have any REAL problems. Well, except for the whole princess thing. And the ihatemiathermopolis.com thing.

But so what? Lots of people get crummy things written about them on the Internet. I mean, look at Rachael Ray, that woman on the Food Network. There's a whole online community devoted to how much people hate her, and she's totally adorable. You can't take it personally. You certainly can't make a big deal out of it. That just gives the haters what they want – the attention they so obviously crave.

And if I tell on them – like if I tell my dad, and he goes to Principal Gupta about it, and she figures out who is doing it and expels them or whatever (because Albert Einstein High School has an online harassment policy that is supposed to protect its students from bullying like this), what good will it do?

They're – whoever they are . . . and let's face it, I have a pretty good idea who 'they' are – just going to hate me more.

Right.

And so my boyfriend dumped me, and I'm still in love with him – so much so, it hurts. Big deal. Millions of girls have gotten dumped by their boyfriends over the years. I'm not special. My own best friend got dumped just like this a couple of weeks ago.

And now the guy who dumped her says he loves me.

Go figure.

That's not why I'm crying either. I guess. I don't know . . .

And poor J.P.! I can't believe I just left him hanging like that. I mean, I didn't give him an answer either way. I just sort of . . . ignored him.

But I have to say *something*, or it's going to be weird.

It's going to be weird either way, of course.

But he took a risk, putting himself out there like that. The least I can do is pay him the common courtesy of responding.

It's just . . . I don't know what to say.

I don't! I mean, I know I don't love him back – obviously.

But that doesn't mean, like Tina said, that I couldn't learn to. If I let myself.

In fact, if I let myself, I have an idea I could love J.P. a lot.

Just, you know. In a different way than I loved Michael.

But maybe I shouldn't be making decisions like this after midnight on a day when I nearly got blown up and almost two weeks after I got dumped and almost one week into cowboy therapy and two nights before I'm supposed to make a speech about drainage in front of two thousand sophisticated New York businesswomen and an hour after I discovered ihatemiathermopolis.com is being written by someone who goes to my school and maybe, possibly could be, my ex-best friend (but it *couldn't* be her, right? That would be *too* mean, even for Lilly).

Maybe I should sleep on it. Maybe I should just go to bed and –

OK. That is never going to work. I am never going to get to sleep unless I –

Dear J.P.

Hi. So . . . today was weird, huh?

And it's probably only going to be weirder tomorrow, what with all these newspapers and stuff saying how Kenny is a psychopathic madman, and you and I are going out and all.

Not that I mind – if I'm going to be falsely romantically linked with anybody, I'm glad it's you. Ha ha.

It's just . . . I don't know if I'm ready yet to be NOT falsely romantically linked with anybody. Do you know what I mean?

Even though it was almost a couple of weeks ago now, it still seems like it was just yesterday that Michael and I broke up. And I'm not sure I'm ready to get back in the saddle and date again –

Oh my God. Dr Knutz isn't even here, and I'm using horse allegories. That is just so wrong.

OK, delete, delete, delete.

Even though it was almost a couple of weeks ago now, it still seems like it was just yesterday that Michael and I broke up. I think I need more time to figure out who I am without him before I hook up with anybody –

Hook up!!! NO NO NO NO!!!! DELETE!!!

I think I need more time to figure out who I am without him before I start going out with somebody else.

OK. Better.

I really do count you as one of my best friends, J.P. And if I WAS going to date anyone this soon, it would be you.

Oh, God. Is that even true? I mean, I *do* like him . . . he's no Michael of course. But who is? Except Michael of course.

But what about Lilly? It's true she's mad at me right now (but she *can't* be behind ihatemiathermopolis.com . . . where would she even find the time, between student government and *Lilly Tells It Like It Is* and dating Kenny and all?) – and I'm not even really sure why.

But what if by some miracle she decides to forgive

me for whatever it is that I did to her? And then she finds out I'm going out with her ex?

On the other hand . . . *she*'s going out with *my* ex.

And, OK, I spent most of the time I was dating Kenny trying to figure out how to break up with him. But still. She can't be mad at me for doing exactly what *she*'s doing . . . can she?

Oh God. I don't know.

I don't know anything any more.

Which leads me to:

But I need to get my head straightened out before I can let anybody else into it. Does that make sense?

Please don't hate me.

Love

Mia

OK. Hitting *Send* before I can change my mind . . .

Thursday, September 23, 7 a.m., the Loft

Inbox: 2!

The first one was from Michael. My heart started beating super fast when I saw it.

But I must be getting a little better, because my
palms didn't get sweaty this time.

Could therapy be working? Or am I just completely
dehydrated from all that crying last night?

I couldn't help wondering, like always, if maybe he'd
finally changed his mind and decided he wanted to get
back together after all . . .

If he did, would I go for it? Would I really stoop that low
and take him back, after everything I've been through
in the past few weeks?

Yeah. I would.

But I was crushed (again) to see it was just a link to
the *New York Post*'s story covering the AEHS explosion
yesterday, with a note that said:

*So I guess Kenny finally figured out how to get the attention he's
always felt he deserves . . .*

Then there was a wink face, and then Michael's signature.

So. I guess he's not upset about all the stuff about me
and J.P. after all.

Not that he would be. Since we're just friends and all.
Sigh.

The second email was from J.P. in response to mine. I have to admit, my heart didn't speed up AT ALL when I saw it.

Dear Mia

You take all the time you need to get your head straightened out (although I have to admit your head's always seemed perfect to me). I'll wait.

Love

J.P.

So. That's nice.
   I guess.

Thursday, September 23, Homeroom

I know I'm not supposed to be writing in my journal at school, but this is just homeroom, and not a real class anyway, so they can't bust me.

And this isn't my journal, which is at home, but my pre-calculus notebook.

And besides, I HAVE to write this down, because I just saw the most random thing. And I'm sure Dr Knutz would want me to write it down for my own SANITY just to process it:

When the limo pulled up to let me off at school – in a special cordoned-off area, because there are still so many reporters and news vans outside the school, trying to get interviews with students and faculty about the 'mad bomber' – I got out and looked around for Lars, who turned out to be standing right next to me, but I totally spaced noticing him because I'm so dazed from lack of sleep.

Anyway, that's how I happened to see, under the scaffolding from where they're replacing the mortar on one of the brick buildings across the street, this tall guy in a black leather jacket, faded jeans and dark sunglasses with a red bandana around his head staring intently at the school.

And at first I was like, *What is Ryan from* The OC *doing across the street from our school? I thought that show got cancelled* . . .

And then the totally weird thing happened: a girl in an AEHS uniform walked up to the guy and tugged on his sleeve . . .

. . . and he turned around and put his arms around her and the two of them started kissing passionately.

And I realized the girl was Lilly Moscovitz, and the hottie in the leather jacket was KENNY SHOW-ALTER!!!!

YES!!! The suspended juvenile delinquent who caused all this trauma in the first place!!! Showing up at school to kiss his girlfriend before classes started!!!!

All of which, of course, begs the question:

When did Kenny Showalter get hot????

And also . . .

WHY WON'T LILLY TALK TO ME????

Because I am totally DYING to ask her how this whole Kenny thing came about in the first place. And also how the student council is going. And if Kenny has shown her his *Final Fantasy* action-figure collection he first started assembling when he and I were going out. And if she's behind ihatemiathermopolis.com, and if so, what I ever did to make her hate me so much.

Also if Michael ever asks about me.

But I can't. Because she wouldn't tell me anyway.

Thursday, September 23, English

Mia! How ARE you?

> I'm fine, Tina! I mean, I'm a little stiff from being knocked to the ground yesterday. But my butt only hurts if I sit on it a certain way.

That's good! But I meant . . . how are you EMOTIONALLY? You know . . . about ihatemia-thermopolis.com. And also J.P., and what he told you.

> Oh! That! Yeah. No big deal. Us celebs have to get used to being cyberhated. And about the J.P. thing, I guess I'm OK. J.P. said he's willing to wait, you know, until I'm ready. To date again. So. That's good.

He's so sweet! And it's so romantic, how he SAVED you, the woman who unleashed his inner-passion volcano. And did you see how hot he looked in that picture on the cover of the *New York Post* this morning, with him in the back of that ambulance looking at you sitting in the back of that other ambulance? Now the whole city wants you date him!

> I know. No pressure.

You know I'm kidding!

> I know, Tina. But that's the thing: it's really true. The problem is . . . I just don't know if *I* want to.

214

Well, whatever you decide, I'll always love you. You know that, right?

Thanks, T. I just wish everyone was as sweet as you.

Thursday, September 23, Gifted and Talented

Lunch was excruciating today. Everyone was coming up and congratulating J.P. for saving me.

Not that I don't think J.P. deserves everybody's praise and thanks.

It's just that . . . that thing Tina said? It's really true. It's like everyone in the world is rooting for J.P. and me to go out – not including everyone who already thinks we ARE going out.

And I feel totally bad for resenting it, because J.P. really is a great guy, and we totally SHOULD be dating.

It's just – how come everybody wasn't this gung-ho about *Michael and me* going out? I mean, sure, Michael never saved me from exploding nitrostarch.

But he saved my sanity PLENTY of times.

And it's not like he's over there in Japan learning how to draw MANGAS or something like that. He's over there building something that's going to save people's *lives*.

Geesh.

Thursday, September 23, PE

Oh my God. I KNEW it was going to happen. I knew there was going to be a price to pay for being chummy with Lana Weinberger:

She's making me cut class with her.

And, OK, the only class I'm missing is PE, which isn't exactly integral to my academic career.

But still! I'm so not a class-ditching type of girl!

Well, I mean, I've ditched . . . but usually only to sit in the third-floor stairwell to talk to someone – generally ME – through an emotional trauma . . . not to go to Starbucks.

But Lana and Trisha were waiting for me in the girls' locker room when I got there today. They grabbed me and hustled me – right past Lars, who'd been leaning against the wall by the water fountain playing Fantasy Football on his cellphone – out of school and down the street (Lars finally caught up around 77th Street). Lana said she really, really needed a non-fat mocha latte, and that she couldn't possibly sit through Spanish (the class she has this period) anyway, because it's right beneath the chem lab, and that whole side of the school still reeks of smoke.

'Besides,' Lana said. 'With all the reporters standing around outside, trying to get interviews with Principal Gupta about Beaker, it's not like we're going to *obtenga cualquier trabajo hecho* anyway.'

Which is no exaggeration. Our school is still the centre of a media blitzkrieg, there are so many news vans and reporters crowded outside (keeping off the school property, however, with the help of the NYPD, whom the school board apparently called in for crowd control) trying to get interviews about 'Beaker the mad bomber'.

However, we managed to get past them without my being recognized, thanks to draping our blazers over our heads and running for it. Which was educational, in that it illustrated how it might feel to have to wear a burka.

'So,' Lana said once we were all seated. 'Everyone's saying that J.P. guy saved your life. Are you two like going out?'

'No,' I said, feeling myself beginning to blush.

'Dude, why not?' Trisha had ordered a non-fat mochacino and was blowing on it to cool it off. 'Saving your life? That's hot.'

'Yeah.' My cheeks felt as warm as my hot chocolate. 'I just – you know. I'm just coming out of a long-term relationship, and I don't know if I'm ready to jump back into another right now.'

'I hear you,' Lana said. 'That's how I've felt ever since I broke up with Josh. We're young, you know? We have to play the field. Who needs to be tied down to one guy when you're SIXTEEN?'

'I'd like to be tied down to Skeet Ulrich,' Trisha volunteered.

'It's just,' I said, ignoring the Skeet Ulrich remark. Although, you know, ditto, 'I really love Michael. And the idea of being with some other guy . . . I don't know. It doesn't do anything for me.'

'I know exactly what you mean,' Lana said, slurping some non-fat foam from her wooden stirrer. 'After Josh and I broke up, I was like, who can ever replace Josh, you know? Because he's like so tall and hot and smart, and good about hanging out in the boyfriend chair while I'm shopping.'

'Totally,' Trisha said, nodding in agreement, 'good about that. A lot of guys aren't. You'd be surprised.'

'So I was really reluctant, you know, to hook up with anyone,' Lana went on, 'because I just didn't want to get hurt again. But then I thought, I need to make a new start. You know? Like a do over. So I went to a party. And that's where I met Blaine.'

'Blaize,' Trisha corrected her.

'Was that his name?' Lana looked far away. 'Oh yeah. Well, whatever. He was like my rebound guy. And after that I was totally cured.'

'You need a rebound guy,' Trisha said, pointing at me with her stirrer.

'I think it should be that J.P. guy,' Lana agreed. 'I mean, he let himself get set on FIRE for you.'

'Getting set on fire is so hot,' Trisha informed me. Apparently without irony.

I nodded anyway. 'I know. The thing is . . . on paper, J.P. is the perfect guy for me. We both love the theatre and movies and come from similar backgrounds and my grandmother totally loves him and we both want to be writers—'

'And you're both always scribbling in those note-books,' Lana said, pointing at my Mead composition notebook with a manicured nail. 'Like you're doing now. Which isn't weird at all, by the way.'

'Yeah,' I said, ignoring Trisha's sarcastic snort. 'And I know he's good-looking and it was cool how he saved me and all. But it's just . . . he doesn't smell right.'

I knew they were both going to stare at me funnily.

And they both did. They had no idea what I was talking about.

No one does. No one gets it.

Except maybe my dad.

'Just get him a different cologne,' Trisha said.

'Yeah,' Lana said. 'Josh used to wear this totally gross stuff that practically gave me a migraine, so for his birthday that year I got him some Drakkar Noir and he started wearing that instead. Problem solved.'

I had to pretend like I was thankful for this tip and that it actually helped. Even though it totally didn't. This, it turns out, is totally the problem with being friends with people in the popular crowd:

You can't always tell them the truth about stuff, because a lot of things they just don't understand.

Thursday, September 23, Chemistry

> Mia – you were so quiet at lunch today. Are you OK?

Yes, J.P.! Fine! Just . . . a little overwhelmed.

> Not because of me, I hope.

No! Nothing to do with you!

You can't tell cute guys the truth about stuff either.

> You're lying.

No! I'm not! What would make you say that?

> Your nostrils are flaring.

DANG! Can NOTHING in my life remain a secret?

Oh. Lilly told you about that?

> She did. Listen, the last thing I want is for things to be weird between us.

They're not! Well, I mean . . . not really.

> I told you – I can wait.

I know! And it's sweet of you. Really sweet!

I'm too sweet, aren't I? Too much of a nice guy? Girls never fall for the nice guys.

No! You're not nice. You're scary, remember? At least according to your therapist . . .

Hey, that's right. And didn't your doctor tell you to do something every day that scares you?

Um. Yes . . .

Then you should go out with me Friday night.

I can't! I have a thing.

Mia. I thought we were going to be honest with each other.

Do you see my nostrils flaring? Seriously, I have to give a speech at this Domina Rei gala.

Fine. I'll be your escort.

You can't. It's women only.

Right.

I'm serious. Believe me, I wish I wasn't.

OK. Saturday then.

I can't! Seriously, I have to study. Do you have any

idea how tenuously I'm hanging on to my B-plus average right now?

> Fine. But sooner or later, I'm taking you out. And you're going to forget all about Michael. I promise.

J.P. You have no idea how much I hope that's true.

Thursday, September 23, 8 p.m., Limo on the way to the Four Seasons

OK. It's really hard to write this because my hands are shaking so hard.

But I need to get it all down. Because something happened.

Something big.

Bigger than a nitrostarch explosion. Bigger than Lilly hating me and maybe possibly being the founder of ihatemiathermopolis.com. Bigger than J.P. turning out to love me. Bigger than Michael turning out NOT to love me (any more). Bigger than me having to start therapy. Bigger than my mom marrying my algebra teacher and having his baby, or me turning out to be a princess, or Michael ever even loving me in the first place.

Bigger than anything that's happened to me ever.

OK. This is what happened:

It started out like a normal enough evening. I mean, I worked with Mr G on my homework (I will never pass either chemistry or pre-calculus without daily tutoring. That much is clear), had dinner, and finally decided, you know, that Lana's right: I need to make a new start. I need a do over. Seriously. It's time to go out with the old – old boyfriends, old best friends, old clothes that don't fit me any more and old decor – and in with the new.

So I was rearranging my bedroom furniture (whatever. I was done with my homework, and I DON'T HAVE A TV ANY MORE. What ELSE was I supposed to do? Look up mean things about myself on the

Internet? There is now a comment section on ihatemia-thermopolis.com, where someone from South Dakota just posted *I hate Mia Thermopolis too! She is so shallow and self-absorbed! I once sent her an email care of the Genovian palace and she never wrote back!*) when I accidentally knocked over Princess Amelie's portrait.

And the back fell off. You know, the wood part that was over the back of the frame?

And I totally freaked out, because you know, that portrait is probably priceless or whatever, like everything else at the palace.

So I scrambled over to pick it up.

And this paper fell out.

Not a paper really. Some parchment. Like the kind they used to write on, back in the 1600s.

And it was covered all over in this scrawly seventeenth-century French that was really hard to read. It took me forever to decipher what it said. I mean, I could see that at the bottom it was signed by Princess Amelie – *my* Princess Amelie. And that right next to her signature was the Genovian royal seal. And that next to that were the signatures of two witnesses, whose names were not familiar to me.

It took me a minute to figure out that they had to be the signatures of the two witnesses she had found to sign off her executive order.

That's when I realized what I was looking at. That thing Amelie had signed – the thing her uncle had gotten so mad at her for, and burned all the copies of . . . except one, that she'd hidden somewhere close to her heart.

At first I'd thought she'd meant LITERALLY next to her heart, and that whatever it was, it must have been

225

burned to a crisp along with Amelie's body in the royal funeral pyre after her death.

But then I realized she hadn't been being literal at all. She'd meant next to her PORTRAIT's heart . . . which, in fact, is where the parchment had fallen – from between the portrait and its backing. Where she'd hidden it to keep her uncle from finding it . . . and where the Genovian parliament was supposed to look for it, after Amelie's diary and the portrait were returned to them from the abbey to which she'd sent them for safe keeping.

Except, of course, no one ever did. Read the diary, I mean (beyond translating it, apparently). Or find the parchment.

Until me.

So then, of course, I wondered what this thing could say. You know, if it had made her uncle so mad he'd tried to burn all the copies, and she'd gone to so much trouble to hide the last one.

And even though at first it was kind of hard to figure out what exactly the document was talking about, by the time I'd finished translating all the words I didn't know with the help of an online medieval French dictionary (thank you, nerds), I had a pretty good idea why Uncle Francesco had been so mad.

And also why Amelie had hidden it. And left clues in her journal as to where it could be found.

Because it was possibly the most inflammatory document I have ever read. Hotter even than Kenny's nitrostarch-synthesis experiment.

For a second I could only stare down at it in total and complete astonishment.

And then I realized something . . . something *amazing*:

Princess Amelie Virginie Renaldo, from all the way back in 1669, had just totally *saved my butt*!!!!!

Not just my butt, but my sanity . . .

    . . . My life . . .

      . . . My future . . .

        . . . My *everything*.

Really. It sounds like I'm exaggerating, and I know I do that a lot, but in this case . . . I'm not. I am totally and completely one hundred per cent heart-pounding sweaty-palmed dry-mouthed serious.

So serious that for a minute I thought I might have a heart attack on the spot.

Which is why as soon as I knew I was actually going to be OK, I called my dad and told him I was on my way uptown to see him. And Grandmere too.

Because I have something to say to both of them.

Friday, September 24, 1 a.m., the Loft

I can't believe this. I can't believe they're –

This isn't happening. It's just NOT HAPPENING. It CAN'T be happening. Because how could my own blood relatives be so . . . so . . . so *horrible*?

I guess I could understand GRANDMERE's reaction. But Dad? My OWN *father*?

It's not like he didn't think about what he was doing either. He took the parchment from me and read it. He checked the seal and signature and everything. He studied it for a long time, while Grandmere sat there sputtering, 'Ridiculous! A Genovian princess, granting the people the right to ELECT a head of state, and declaring that the role of the Genovian sovereign is one of ceremony only? No ancestor of ours would be that stupid.'

'Amelie wasn't being stupid, Grandmere,' I explained to her. 'What she did was actually really smart. She was trying to HELP the Genovian people, by sparing them from being ruled by someone she knew from personal experience was a tyrant, and who was only going to make an already bad situation, with the plague and everything, worse. It's just bad luck that no one found the document until now.'

'It certainly is,' Dad said, still studying the parchment. 'It might have spared the Genovian people a lot of hardship. The fact is, Princess Amelie made what, under the circumstances, was the best decision she could make at that time.'

'Right,' I said. 'So we'll have to get this to Parliament as soon as possible. They'll want to start nominating candidates for prime minister and figure out when they're going to hold elections as soon as possible. And, Dad, I was going to say, I know this must come as a total blow to you, but if I know the Genovian people – and I think I do by now – there's only one person they're going to want as their prime minister, and that's you.'

'That's kind of you to say, Mia,' Dad said.

'Well, it's true,' I said. 'And there's nothing in the Bill of Rights as Amelie has laid them out to preclude any member of the royal family from running for prime minister if he or she wants to. So I think you should go for it. I know it's not exactly the same thing, but I have some experience with elections thanks to the student-council race last year. So if you need any help, I'll be glad to do whatever I can.'

'What is this?' Grandmere sputtered. 'Has everyone gone completely mad? Prime minister? No son of mine is going to be a prime minister! He's a prince, need I remind you, Amelia!'

'Grandmere.' I know it's really hard sometimes for old people to adjust to new things – like the Internet – but I knew Grandmere would catch on eventually. She's a real pro with a mouse now. 'I know Dad's a prince. And he'll always stay one. Just like you'll always be dowager princess and I'll always be a princess. It's just that, according to Amelie's declaration, Genovia's no longer *ruled* by a prince or princess. It's led by an elected parliament and headed by an elected prime minister—'

'That is ridiculous!' Grandmere cried. 'I did not spend all this time teaching you how to be princess only to have it turn out you're NOT one after all!'

'Grandmere.' Seriously. You'd think she'd never taken a Government class before. 'I'm still a princess.

Just a ceremonial one. Like Princess Aiko of Japan . . . or Princess Beatrice in England. Both England and Japan are constitutional monarchies . . . like Monaco.'

'Monaco!' Grandmere looked horrified. 'Good God in heaven, Philippe! We can't be like *Monaco*. What is she saying?'

'Nothing, Mother,' Dad said. I hadn't noticed before, but his jaw was squared. That is always a sign – like Mom's mouth getting small – that things are not about to go my way. 'It's nothing for you to worry about.'

'Well, actually,' I said, 'it *is*. I mean, a little. It's going to be a pretty big change. But only in a good way, I think. Our membership of the European Union was on pretty shaky ground before because of the whole absolute monarchy thing, right? I mean, remember the snails? But now, as a democracy—'

'Democracy, again!' Grandmere cried. 'Philippe! What does all this mean? What is she TALKING about? Are you, or are you not, the Prince of Genovia?'

'Of course I am, Mother,' Dad said in a soothing voice. 'Don't get excited. Nothing's going to change. Let me ring for a Sidecar for you . . .'

I totally understood Dad trying to calm Grandmere down and all. But outright lying to her seemed a little cold.

'Well,' I said 'actually, a *lot* is going to change—'

'No,' Dad interrupted briskly. 'No, Mia, actually, it's not. I appreciate your bringing this document to my attention, but it doesn't actually mean what you seem to think it means. It doesn't have any validity.'

That's when my jaw dropped. 'WHAT? Of *course* it does! Amelie completely followed all the rules laid out in the Genovian royal charter – used the seal and got the signature of two unrelated witnesses and everything! If I've learned anything since my princess lessons started, I've learned that. It's valid.'

'But she didn't have parliamentary approval,' Dad began.

'BECAUSE EVERYONE IN PARLIAMENT WAS DEAD!' I couldn't believe this. 'Or at home, nursing their dying relatives. And, Dad, you know as well as I do that in a national crisis – like, for instance, a PLAGUE, a ruler's impending death, and her knowledge that her throne is going to a known despot – a crowned Genovian prince or princess can sign into law anything he or she wants to, by order of divine right.'

Seriously. Does he really think I've learned NOTHING but how to use a fish fork in two years of princess lessons?

'Right,' Dad said. 'But this particular national crisis was nearly four hundred years ago, Mia.'

'That doesn't make this bill any less valid,' I insisted.

'No,' Dad admitted. 'But it does mean there's no reason we have to share it with Parliament at this time. Or any time, really.'

'*WHAT?*'

Seriously. I felt like Princess Leia Organa when she finally revealed the hidden location of the rebel base (even though she was lying) to Grand Moff Tarkin in *Star Wars: A New Hope*, and he went ahead and ordered the destruction of her home planet of Alderaan anyway.

'Of *course* we have to share it,' I yelled. 'Dad, Genovia has been living a lie for almost four hundred years!'

'This conversation is over,' Dad said, taking Amelie's Bill of Rights and getting ready to slide it into his briefcase. 'I appreciate the attempt, Mia – it was very clever of you to figure it all out. But this is hardly a legitimate legal document that we need to bring to the attention of the Genovian people – or Parliament. It's merely an attempt by a scared teenaged girl to protect the interests of a people who are long since dead, and nothing we need to worry about—'

'That's just it,' I said. I hurried over and took the parchment before he could seal it away forever in the darkness of his Gucci bag. I was starting to cry. I couldn't help it. It was all just so unfair. 'Isn't it? That it's written by a *girl*. Worse, that it's written by a *TEENAGED girl*. So therefore, it has no legitimacy and can just be ignored—'

Dad gave me a sour look. 'Mia, you know that's not what I mean.'

'Yes it is! If this had been written by one of our MALE ancestors – Prince Francesco himself perhaps – you'd totally have presented it to Parliament when they meet in session next month. TOTALLY. But because it was written by a teenaged girl, who was only princess for twelve days before she died horribly and all alone, you plan on completely disregarding it. Does the freedom of your own people really mean so little to you?'

'Mia,' Dad said, sounding weary. 'Genovia is consistently rated among the best places to live on the *planet*, and the Genovian population the most contented. The median temperature is seventy-two degrees, it's sunny almost three hundred days of the year, and no one there pays any taxes, remember? Genovians have certainly never expressed the slightest reserve about their freedom, or lack of it, since I've been on the throne.'

'How can they miss what they've never had, Dad?' I

asked him. 'And that's not even the point. The point is that one of your ancestors left behind a legacy – something she intended to be used to protect the people she cared about. Her uncle threw it away, the same way he tried to throw *her* away. If we don't honour her last request, we're every bit as bad as he was.'

Dad rolled his eyes. 'Mia. It's late. I'm going back to my suite. We'll talk about this some more tomorrow. If,' I distinctly heard him mutter, 'you haven't gotten over it by then.'

Which really gets to the heart of the matter, doesn't it? He thinks I'm just suffering from some adolescent female histrionics . . . the same kind that prompted him to put me into therapy, and Princess Amelie into signing that bill in the first place.

The bill he is ignoring because – basically – a girl wrote it.

Nice. Really nice.

And Grandmere was no help whatsoever. I mean, you would think a fellow woman would have some sympathy for my – and Amelie's – plight.

But Grandmere is just like all those other women who go around wanting the same rights as men, but don't want to call themselves feminists. Because that isn't 'feminine'.

After Dad left, she just looked at me and was like, 'Well, Amelia, I'm still not sure what all that was about, but I told you not to bother with that dusty old diary. Now, are you ready for your speech tomorrow? Your suit has been delivered here, so I suppose the best thing would be for you to come straight over after school and change here.'

'I can't come straight over after school,' I said to her. 'I have therapy tomorrow.'

She blinked at me a few times – I was never sure how much Dad has told her about Dr Knutz. But now I know it's nothing – and went, 'Well. After that then.'

!!!!!

Seriously. My grandmother finds out I'm in therapy, and all she says is for me to come over AFTERWARDS to change for the speech I am ONLY giving because SHE wants to be a Domina Rei.

I could kill both of them right now. Dad AND Grandmere.

I came home so mad I couldn't even speak. I just went into my room and shut the door.

Not that Mom or Mr G even noticed. They finally got all the seasons so far of *The Wire* on Netflix and are glued to the TV.

The TV in their BEDROOM.

Because no one took THEIR TV away.

I thought about going in there and telling them – well, Mom, anyway – what was going on. Except that I knew the information would cause her head to explode. Her former boyfriend and his mother, robbing a woman of her basic human rights (because that's what Dad and Grandmere are doing to Amelie really)? Mom would be *so* on the warpath. She would get all her Riot Grrls on the phone and be down picketing the Genovian Embassy in no time. Then if that didn't work, she'd karate chop Dad in the neck (she's been working off her leftover pregnancy weight and is back up to her brown belt).

Except.

Except that's not what I want.

For one thing, domestic violence is never the answer.

And for another, I don't want my MOM to fix this. I need advice on how *I* can fix this. ME.

I can't believe any of this. Can this actually – truly – be my life?

And if so . . . how did this *happen*?

Friday, September 24, English

Mia! Are you all right? You look like you didn't get much sleep last night!

Yeah. That'd be because I didn't.

Why???? Oh my gosh, did something happen with J.P.? Or MICHAEL???

Ha. No, Tina. Believe it or not, this has nothing to do with a boy. Well, except my dad.

Did he give you that speech again about how if you don't study harder you won't get into an Ivy League school and then you'll end up married to a circus performer like your cousin Princess Stéphanie? Because I've been meaning to say, I really think MOST people don't end up getting into Ivy League schools, and very few of them end up married to contortionists, so I don't think this is a very valid concern.

No. It's worse than that.

Oh my God, did he find out about how you were going to give your Precious Gift to Michael??? Except Michael didn't want it????

No. Something way, way more important . . .

More important than your Precious Gift? What is
it then????????

Well –

I will not pass notes in class.
I will not pass notes in class.
I will not pass notes in class.
I will not pass notes in class.
I will not pass notes in class.
I will not pass notes in class.
I will not pass notes in class.
I will not pass notes in class.
I will not pass notes in class.
I will not pass notes in class.
I will not pass notes in class.
I will not pass notes in class.
I will not pass notes in class.
I will not pass notes in class.
I will not pass notes in class.
I will not pass notes in class.
I will not pass notes in class.
I will not pass notes in class.
I will not pass notes in class.
I will not pass notes in class.
I will not pass notes in class.
I will not pass notes in class.

Friday, September 24, Lunch Period, Third-Floor Stairwell

I don't even know what to say. I bet the words on this page are all smeary from my tears.

Only I'm crying so hard I can't tell, since I can barely see the page anyway.

I just – I just don't understand how she could have SAID that.

Let alone DONE that.

I don't even know what I was thinking.

It's just that this is so much WORSE than the fact that my long-time boyfriend has dumped me. Worse than my best friend's ex claiming to be in love with me. Worse than the fact that my former enemy now sits with me at lunch. Worse than the fact that I'm barely passing pre-calc.

I mean, my father is trying to bilk the Genovian people out of their one shot at being a democratic society.

And there's really only a single person I know who can tell me what I actually ought to do about all this (instead of, like my mom, taking over and doing it all herself).

And she's not speaking to me.

But I thought we could rise above the petty stuff. I really thought we could.

Seriously. I just felt like I *needed* to talk to Lilly. Because Lilly would know what I should do.

And what, I thought, would be the worst thing that could happen if I just TOLD her? What if I just walked up and *told* her what was going on? She'd HAVE to respond, right? Because it's such an injustice, she wouldn't be able to help it. She's LILLY. Lilly can't stand idly by while an injustice is being perpetrated. She's physically incapable of it. She'd HAVE to say something.

And most likely, what she'd say is, 'You have GOT to be kidding me. Mia, you have to –'

And then she'd tell me what to do. Right?

And then I'd be able to stop feeling like I'm sliding further and further down Papaw's cistern.

I mean, maybe we wouldn't be friends again.

But Lilly would never let a country be cheated out of government by the people. Right? As opposed as she is to the monarchy.

That was my reasoning, anyway. That's why I went up to her just now in the cafeteria.

I swear that's all I did. I just walked over to her. That's all. All I did was go over to where she was sitting – ALONE, by the way, because Kenny is suspended, and Perin was off at an orthodontist's appointment, and Ling Su had chosen to stay in the art room to finish a collage of herself she's calling *Portrait of the Artist in Ramen Noodles and Olives* – and go, 'Lilly? Can I talk to you a second?'

And OK, maybe it was a bad idea to approach her in public. I probably should have waited in the Girls' Room, since she always goes in there when she's done eating. Then I could have talked to her in private, and if she reacted badly no one would have seen or heard it but me, and maybe a few freshmen.

But like an IDIOT I went up to her in front of everyone and slid into the seat across from hers and went, 'Lilly, I know you're not speaking to me, but I really need your help. Something terrible has happened: I found out that nearly four hundred years ago one of my ancestresses signed a bill making Genovia a constitutional monarchy, but no one found the bill until the other day, and when I showed it to my dad he basically dismissed it because it was written by a teenage girl who only ruled for twelve days before succumbing to the plague, and besides which, he doesn't want a merely ceremonial role in the Genovian government, even though I *told* him he could run for prime minister. You know everyone would vote for him. And I just feel like this enormous injustice is being done, but I don't know what I can do about it, and you're so smart, I figured you could help me –'

Lilly looked up from her salad and went, coldly, 'Why are you even speaking to me?'

Which, I will admit, kind of threw me. I probably should have gotten up and walked away right then and there.

But, like the idiot that I am, I kept going. Because . . . I don't know. We've been through so much together, I just figured maybe she hadn't heard me right or something.

'I told you,' I said. 'I need your help. Lilly, this whole cold-shoulder thing, it's so stupid.'

She just stared at me some more. So I went, 'Well, OK, if you feel like you have to go on hating me, that's fine. What about the people of Genovia though? They never did anything to you – although neither did I, but that's not the point. Don't you think the people of Genovia deserve to be free to choose their own leader? Lilly, they need you – *I* need you, to help me figure out how to—'

'Oh. My. God.'

Lilly stood up on the word *Oh*. She raised her fist on the word *My*. And she brought it down hard on the table top on the word *God*.

So hard that every single head in the caff swivelled towards us to see what was going on.

'I cannot believe this,' Lilly yelled. Literally, yelled at me, even though I was sitting right across from her, barely two feet away. 'You are completely unbelievable. First you break my brother's heart. Then you steal my boyfriend. Then you think you can ask me for advice about your completely dysfunctional family?'

By the time she got to the word *family*, she was screaming.

I just blinked up at her, completely shocked. Also, not able to see very well, thanks to the tears in my eyes.

But probably that was good. Because I couldn't see all the stricken faces that were turned in our direction.

Although I could hear the total silence that was roaring across the caff. You couldn't even hear a fork scrape. That's how anxious everyone was to take in every second of the tongue-lashing I was getting from my former best friend.

'Lilly,' I whispered, 'you know I didn't break Michael's heart. He broke mine. And I did *not* steal your boyfriend—'

'Oh, save it for the *New York Post*,' Lilly shouted. 'Nothing is EVER your fault, is it, Mia? But then why should you ever admit you were in the wrong, when the victim thing is working so well for you, right? I mean, look at you. You've got LANA WEINBERGER as your best friend now. Isn't that SPECIAL? Don't you realize that she's just USING you, you idiot? They're all just *using* you, Mia. I was your only real friend, and look how you treated me!'

All I could see of Lilly was a big blur after that, because the tears were coming so fast. But I could hear the contempt in her voice. Also, the complete and utter silence of everyone around us.

'And you know what,' Lilly went on acidly – and still loudly enough to wake the dead. 'You're right. You *didn't* break Michael's heart. He was so sick of your constant whining and complete inability to solve your own problems, he couldn't wait to get away from you. I just wish I was as lucky as he is! I'd give anything to be thousands of miles away from you too. But in the meantime, at least I have the new website I've designed to comfort me. Perhaps you've seen it? If not let me give you the URL – it's IHATEMIATHERMOPOLISDOTCOM!'

And with that, she whirled around and left the cafeteria.

Or at least, I suppose she did. It was kind of hard to tell, since I couldn't actually see what was happening, because by that time I was crying so hard it looked like Niagara Falls was coming down my *face*.

Which was how I didn't notice that Tina and Boris and J.P. and Shameeka and Lana and Trisha had hurried over to where I was sitting until they were patting me on the back and saying things like, 'Don't listen to her, Mia, she didn't mean it,' and, 'She's just jealous. She always has been,' and, 'Nobody's using you, Mia. Because to be honest, you don't really have anything I want.' (This last came from Lana. Who meant it kindly, I know.)

I knew they were just trying to be nice. I knew they just wanted to make me feel better.

But it was too late. Lilly's total annihilation of me –
in such a public manner – was the straw that broke the
camel's entire spinal column. And the fact that Lilly –
Lilly, of all people! – was behind that stupid website?

I guess I always knew it.

But to hear her admit it like that – so proudly, like
she *wanted* me to know . . .

I had to get out of there. I knew by doing so I was just
being what Lilly had accused me of being – a whiny
victim.

But I really needed to just be alone.

Which is what I'm doing here in the third-floor stairwell, which leads to the locked roof door, and where no
one ever goes . . .

No one but Lilly and me, that is, when we've been
upset about something in the past.

Lars is standing guard at the bottom of the stairs to
keep anyone from coming up. He seems genuinely concerned about me. He went, 'Princess, should I call your
mother?'

I was like, 'No thanks, Lars.'

And then he was all, 'Well then, your father, maybe?'

And I was like, 'NO!'

He looked kind of taken aback by my vehemence.
But I was afraid he was going to ask if he should call Dr
Knutz next.

Thankfully though, he just nodded and said, 'All
right then. If you're sure . . .'

Am I ever sure. I told him I just needed to be by
myself for a little while. I said I'd be right back down . . .

But it's been fifteen minutes, and I don't feel like the
tears are going to stop any time soon. I just – how could
she *say* those things? After everything we've been

through together? How could she WRITE those things on her site? How can she think I would ever do anything like what she accused me of? How could she ever be so . . . so *cruel*?

Oh no. I hear footsteps. Lars is letting someone up! WHY, LARS, WHY???? I told you –

Friday, September 24, Gifted and Talented

Oh God. That was so . . .

Random.

Really. That's the only word I can think of to describe it.

Which makes it no wonder Ms Martinez despairs of my ever being a successful freelance writer or journalist.

But seriously! How else can I put it? It was just . . . RANDOM.

And what was Lars THINKING? I told him to let NO ONE up. Except for Principal Gupta or a teacher, OBVIOUSLY.

So how did BORIS become exempt from that?

But sure enough, I heard footsteps on the stairs, and the next thing I knew, BORIS was there, all out of breath, like he'd been running.

At first I was worried he was going to tell me HE loves me too (well, whatever, it's amazing the things that start happening when you finally grow into a 36C).

But fortunately he just went, 'There you are. I've been looking for you all over. Look, I'm not supposed to tell you this, but it's not true.'

'*What*'s not true, Boris?' I asked him, totally confused.

'What Lilly just said,' he said. 'About Michael being sick of you. I can't tell you how I know. But I do.'

I smiled at him. Even though I was still in total despair and everything, I couldn't help it. Really, Tina is so lucky. She has the most fantastic boyfriend in the entire world.

Fortunately, she knows it.

'Thanks, Boris,' I said, trying to wipe away my tears with my sleeve so I didn't look like quite as much of a lunatic as I was pretty sure I did. 'That's really sweet of you to say.'

'I'm not being sweet,' Boris insisted earnestly, still panting from all the running around he'd been doing, looking for me. 'I'm telling the truth. And you should write him back.'

I blinked at him, more confused than ever. 'W-what? Write who back?'

'Michael,' Boris said. 'He's been emailing you, right?'

'Yeah,' I said, stunned. 'But how did you—'

'You should write him back,' Boris said. 'I mean, just because you're broken up doesn't mean you can't be friends any more. Isn't that what you both agreed? That you'd still be friends?'

'Yes,' I said bewilderedly. 'But, Boris, how do you know he's been emailing me? Did . . . did Tina tell you?'

Boris hesitated, then nodded. 'Yes. That's right, Tina told me.'

'Oh,' I said. 'Well, I can't email him back, Boris. I'm just . . . I'm not ready to be friends with him yet. It still hurts too much not to be *more* than friends.'

'Well,' Boris said. 'I can understand that, I guess. But . . . you should email him back as soon as you feel ready. So he doesn't think – you know. That you hate him. Or that you've forgotten about him. Or whatever.'

As if THAT'S ever going to happen.

I assured Boris I'd email Michael when I felt emotionally capable of doing so without falling apart and begging him in eighteen-point type to take me back.

Then Boris did the nicest thing. He volunteered to

247

walk me to class (once I'd pulled myself together and gotten rid of the evidence of my tears . . . smeared mascara, snot down my nose, etc.).

So the three of us – Boris, Lars and I – all got to G and T at the same time (late).

But it didn't matter, since neither Mrs Hill nor Lilly is here.

I suppose Lilly's skipping to meet Kenny somewhere. They're like a regular Courtney Love and Kurt Cobain. Minus the heroin. All Lilly needs is to start smoking though, and maybe get a tattoo or two, and she'll have completely perfected her tough-girl image.

Boris asked me one last time if I was all right, and when I said I thought I was, he slipped into the supply closet and started practising my favorite Chopin piece.

Which has to have been on purpose. He's so thoughtful.

Tina really is a lucky girl.

I just hope some day I can be as lucky as she is.

Or maybe I've already *had* my luck where boys are concerned, and I completely squandered and wasted it.

God, I hope that's not the case. Although if it is, all I can say is, it was good while it lasted.

Friday, September 24, Dr Knutz's Waiting Room

Lana and Trisha insisted on taking me out for what they like to call a Mani-Pedi Time-Out. They said I deserved it, after what Lilly did to me in the caff.

So instead of playing softball during sixth period, I got my toenails and what was left of my fingernails (I haven't had new acrylic tips put on since I got back from Genovia this summer, and I've been biting what remains of my natural nails) painted I'm Not Really A Waitress red, a colour Grandmere insists is totally inappropriate for young girls.

Which is precisely why I picked it.

But I have to admit, after we were done with our forty-five-minute manicures/pedicures, I didn't feel much better. I know Lana and Trisha were trying.

But there's just too much drama in my life right now for a simple hand and foot massage (and nail colour application) to cure.

Oh. Dr Knutz is ready to see me now.

I don't think anyone, even Dr Knutz, could EVER be ready for me and the disaster that is my life.

Friday, September 24, Limo on the way to the Four Seasons

So I poured my heart out to Dr Knutz, the cowboy therapist, and here is what he said:

'But Genovia already has a prime minister.'

I just looked at him. 'No, it doesn't,' I said.

'Yes it does,' Dr Knutz said. 'I watched the movies of your life, like you told me to. And I distinctly remember—'

'The movies of my life got that part WRONG,' I said. 'Among the many, many other parts they got wrong. They claimed artistic licence or something. They said they had to raise the stakes. As if the stakes in my REAL life aren't high enough.'

So then Dr Knutz said, 'Oh. I see.' He thought about it for a minute. Then he said, 'You know, all this reminds me of a horse I have, back at the ranch . . .'

I nearly flung myself out of my chair at him.

'DO NOT TELL ME ABOUT DUSTY AGAIN,' I yelled. 'I ALREADY KNOW ABOUT DUSTY!'

'This isn't about Dusty,' Dr Knutz said, looking startled. 'It's about Pancho.'

'How many horses do you have anyway?' I demanded.

'Oh, a few dozen,' Dr Knutz said. 'But that's not important. What's important is, Pancho is a bit of a pushover. Anybody who takes him out of his stall and saddles him up, Pancho falls in love with. He'll rub his head against them, just like a cat, and follow them around . . . even if they don't treat him particularly nicely. Pancho is desperate for affection, wants everybody to like him—'

'OK,' I interrupted. 'I get it. Pancho has self-esteem issues. I do too. But what does this have to do with the fact that my father is trying to keep Princess Amelie's Bill of Rights from the Genovian people?'

'Nothing,' Dr Knutz said. 'It has to do with the fact that you're not trying to do anything to stop him.'

I stared at him some more. 'How am I supposed to do *that*?'

'Well, that's for you to figure out,' Dr Knutz said.

OK. *That* got me mad.

'You said the first day I sat in here,' I yelled, 'that the only way I was going to get out from the bottom of the dark hole of depression I've fallen into was to ask for help. Well, I'm asking you for help . . . and now you tell me I have to figure it out myself? How much are you getting paid an hour for this, anyway?'

Dr Knutz regarded me calmly from behind his notepad.

'Listen to what you've just told me about your day,' he said. 'The boy you love told you he just wants to be friends, and you did nothing. Your best friend humiliated you in front of the entire school, and you did nothing. Your father tells you he isn't honouring the wishes of your dead ancestor, and you do nothing. I told you the first time we met, no one can help you unless you help yourself. Nothing's ever going to change for you if you don't do something every day that—'

'– scares me,' I said. 'I KNOW. But how? What am I *supposed* to do about all this?'

'It isn't about what you're *supposed* to do, Mia,' Dr Knutz said, sounding a little frustrated. 'What do you *want* to do?'

251

I still didn't get it. I was like, 'I want . . . I want . . . I want to do the right thing!'

'That's what I'm telling you,' Dr Knutz said. 'If you want to do the right thing, don't be like Pancho. Do what Princess Amelie would do!'

WHAT WAS HE *TALKING* ABOUT???

But before I had a chance to figure it out, he went, 'Oh, look at that. Our time is up. But this has been a very interesting session. Next week, I'd like to see you with your father again. I have a feeling you two will have some issues that need discussing. And bring along this grandmother of yours,' Dr Knutz added. 'I saw a photo of her on Google. She seems an intriguing woman.'

'Wait a minute,' I said. 'What are you saying? How can I do what Princess Amelie did? Princess Amelie failed. Her bill never got passed. No one ever even KNEW about it. No one but me.'

'Bye for now,' Dr Knutz said.

And shooed me away.

I just don't get it. My dad is paying this guy to help me with my problems. But all he's doing is passing the buck, saying I have to solve my own problems.

But isn't that what he's getting paid for doing???

And how in God's name am I supposed to do anything about the Princess Amelie situation? I made my case to Dad, and he totally blew me off. What more can I do?

The worst part of it is, Dr Knutz got my blood work back from Dr Fung's office. The results? Normal. I'm totally normal, in every regard. *Better* than normal. Like Rocky, I'm in the freaking ninety-ninth percentile for my age group, or something. I was hoping at the very least that the fact I'd started eating meat again would have raised my cholesterol to the point that it could be blamed for my hideous depression.

But my cholesterol is fine. *Everything* is fine. I'm healthy as a freaking horse.

Ouch. Why did I have to use the word horse?

Oh God. We're here. I can't **BELIEVE** I have to do this stupid Domina Rei thing tonight.

All I can say is, if I get Grandmere into this club or whatever it is, she'd better get off my back about my hair.

Pancho? He seriously told me a story about a horse named **PANCHO**?

Friday, September 24, 9 p.m., Ladies' Room, the Waldorf=Astoria

She hates the nail polish.

She's acting like my wearing it is going to totally ruin her chances of being asked to join this crazy club. She's more upset about my nail polish than she is about the fact that our family, for centuries now, has essentially been living a lie. It was the first thing I brought up when I got to her suite.

'Grandmere,' I said. 'You can't agree with Dad that ignoring Princess Amelie Virginie's dying wish is the right thing to do. Can you?'

And she'd rolled her eyes and gone, 'Not that again! Your father PROMISED me you'd have forgotten all about that by now.'

Yeah. I noticed that by how he hadn't returned a single one of my phone calls all day. He was giving me the silent treatment, the same as Lilly.

Well, the same as Lilly until she'd exploded this afternoon, that is.

'But, honestly, Amelia,' Grandmere had gone on. 'You can't expect us to completely alter our lives because of the whim of some four-hundred-year dead princess, can you?'

'Amelie didn't craft her Bill of Rights on a whim, Grandmere. And our lives wouldn't be altered,' I'd insisted. 'We'd still go on just like before. Only we wouldn't actually be RULING. We'd be letting the PEOPLE rule – or at least CHOOSE who they WANT to rule. Which could very well be Dad, you know—'

'But supposing it ISN'T?' Grandmere had demanded. 'Where would we LIVE?'

'Grandmere,' I'd said. 'We'll go on living in the palace as always—'

'No, we wouldn't,' Grandmere had said. 'The palace would become the residence of the prime minister – whoever that would end up being. Do you really think I could stand to see some POLITICIAN living in my beautiful palace? He'll probably have the whole place carpeted. In BEIGE.'

Seriously. I'd wanted to wring her neck. 'Grandmere. The prime minister would live – well, I don't know. But someplace else. We'd still be the royal family and still live in the palace and continue doing all the duties we normally do – *EXCEPT RULING*.'

All she'd had to say to that was, 'Well, your father won't hear of THAT. So you might as well drop it. Really, Amelia, RED nails? Are you trying to give me a stroke?'

Which, all right: I'll admit this evening seems really important to her. You should have seen how she preened when the Contessa came up to me during the cocktail hour and was like, 'Princess Amelia? My goodness! How you've grown since I last saw you!'

'Yes,' Grandmere said acidly, glancing at Bella Trevanni's ginormous stomach. Or should I say, Princess René's ginormous stomach. 'As has your granddaughter.'

'Due any day now,' the Contessa cooed.

'Did you hear?' Bella asked us. 'It's a girl!'

We both congratulated her. She really does look happy – even glowing, the way they always say pregnant women do.

And it totally serves my cousin René right, the fact that he's having a girl, when he himself was always such a flirt. When his kid starts dating, he's finally going to find out how all the fathers of the girls he went out with must have felt.

But the Contessa's not the only person Grandmere's hoping to impress. The crème de la crème of New York society is here – well, the women. No men are allowed at Domina Rei functions, except their annual ball, which this isn't. I just saw Gloria Vanderbilt putting on her lipgloss over by a potted palm.

And I'm pretty sure that Madeleine Albright is adjusting her pantyhose in the stall next to mine.

And look: I get it. I really do get why Grandmere is so anxious to be one of these women. They're all super powerful – and charming too. Lana's mom, Mrs Weinberger, was way nice to me when we first came in – she didn't seem at all like a lady who would sell her daughter's pony without letting her say goodbye – shaking my hand and telling me what an excellent role model I am to young girls everywhere. She said she wished her own daughter had as good a head on her shoulders as I do.

This caused Lana, who was standing next to her mom, to snicker into her tulle stole.

But I realized there were no hard feelings when a second later Lana took me by the arm and said, 'Check it out. They have a chocolate fountain over at the buffet. Only it's low cal, because it's made with Splenda,' then added, when she'd dragged me out of earshot of her mom and Grandmere, 'Also, they've got the hottest busboys you've ever seen.'

Anyway. I'm supposed to give my talk any minute

now. Grandmere made me go over it with her in the limo. I kept telling her it's way too boring to impress anyone, let alone inspire them. But she keeps insisting drainage is what the women of the Domina Rei want to hear about.

Yeah. Because I'm so sure Beverly Bellerieve – of the prime-time news show *Twenty-Four/Seven* – wants to hear all about Genovia's sewage issues. I saw her out in the lobby just now, and she smiled at me all big and said, 'Well, hello there! Don't you look grown up!' I guess remembering that time in my freshman year when we did that interview and –

Oh my God.

OH MY GOD.

No. That is NOT what he meant when he told me – in no way did he mean . . .

No. Just . . .

But wait a minute. He said *not* to be like Pancho. He *said* to do what Princess Amelie would do.

She meant for Genovia to be a democracy.

Only no one knew that.

But that's not true. SOMEone does know.

I know.

And right now, at this very moment, I am in the unique position of being able to let a couple of thousand businesswomen know as well.

Including Beverly Bellerieve, who has the biggest mouth in broadcast journalism.

No. Just no. That would be wrong. That would – that would –

My dad would KILL me.

But . . . that would *definitely* not be like Pancho of me.

But how can I? How can I do that to my dad? To Grandmere?

Well, who cares about Grandmere. How can I do that to my dad?

Oh no. I hear Grandmere – she's coming to get me. It's time –

No! I'm not ready! I don't know what to do! Someone needs to tell me what to do!

Oh God.

I think someone already did.

It's just that it's someone who's been dead for nearly four hundred years.

Princess Drops Bomb
of Different Kind

Princess Mia of Genovia – most recently in the news after a brush with nitrostarch in her Albert Einstein High School chemistry lab sent her and two others (including the princess's rumoured royal-consort-of-the-moment, John Paul Reynolds-Abernathy IV) to Lenox Hill Emergency Room with minor injuries – has dropped an explosive of her own:

That a newly discovered four-hundred-year-old document reveals that the principality of Genovia is a constitutional, not absolute, monarchy.

The difference is a significant one. In an absolute monarchy, the viceroy – in Genovia's case, Princess Mia's father, Prince Artur Christoff Philippe Gerard Grimaldi Renaldo – possesses the divine right to rule over his people and land. In a constitutional monarchy, the ceremonial role of a royal heir (such as the Queen of England) is acknowledged, but all actual governmental decisions are made by an elected head of state, usually in conjunction with a parliamentary body.

Princess Mia made this startling revelation at a gala to benefit African orphans given by Domina Rei, the exclusive women's organization known for its charitable good works and high-profile membership (including Oprah Winfrey and Hillary Clinton).

Princess Mia, in an address to the New York chapter, read a roughly translated selection from the diary of a princess of whom she is a royal descendant, describing the young woman's battle with the plague and an autocratic uncle, and her drawing up and signing of a Bill of Rights guaranteeing the people of Genovia the freedom to elect their next leader.

Unfortunately the document was lost to the ages in the chaos following the plague's deadly journey up and down the Mediterranean coast – lost until now, that is.

Princess Mia's description of her delight in being able to bring democracy to the people of Genovia is said to have brought tears to the eyes of many members of the audience. And her reference to a famous quote by Eleanor Roosevelt – herself a Domina Rei – brought the princess's audience to their feet in a standing ovation.

'Do one thing every day that

frightens you,' Princess Mia advised her audience. 'And never think that you can't make a difference. Even if you're only sixteen and everyone is telling you that you're just a silly teenaged girl – don't let them push you away. Remember one other thing Eleanor Roosevelt said: *No one can make you feel inferior without your consent.* You are capable of great things – never let anyone try to tell you that, just because you've only been a princess for twelve days, you don't know what you're doing.'

'It was totally inspiring,' commented Beverly Bellerieve, star of the news-journal television show *Twenty-Four/Seven*, who has announced plans to devote an entire segment of her show to the small country's transition from monarchy to democracy. 'And the way the Dowager Princess Clarisse, Mia's grandmother, reacted – with open, nearly hysterical, weeping – left not a dry eye in the house. It was truly a night to remember . . . and definitely the best speech we've ever had at a gala, that I can remember.'

Neither the Dowager Princess nor her granddaughter was available for comment, having being whisked away in a limo to destinations unknown immediately following the event.

Calls to the Genovian Palace press office and Prince Philippe were still unanswered at press time.

Friday, September 24, 11 p.m., Limo on the way home from the Four Seasons

You know what? I don't care.

I really don't. I did the right thing. I know I did.

And Dad can yell all he wants – and go on saying that I've ruined all our lives.

And Grandmere can swoon on that couch and call for all the Sidecars she wants.

I don't regret it.

And I never will.

You should have HEARD how quiet that audience got when I started telling them about Amelie Virginie! It was quieter in that banquet room than it was in the school cafeteria today, when Lilly ripped me a new one in front of everyone.

And there were about one thousand six hundred more people in the room tonight than there were this afternoon!

And every single one of them was gazing up at me, totally enraptured by the story of Princess Amelie. I think I saw TEARS in Rosie O'Donnell's eyes – TEARS! – when I got to the part about Uncle Francesco burning the books in the palace library.

And when I got to the part about Amelie discovering her first pustule – I TOTALLY heard a sob from Nancy Pelosi's direction.

But then when I was describing how it's about time the world recognized that sixteen-year-old girls are capable of so much more than wearing some navel-baring outfit on the cover of *Rolling Stone*, or passing out from partying too much in front of some nightclub . . .

and can achieve fame for taking a stand and coming to the aid of a people in need . . .

Well. That's when I got the standing ovation.

I was basking in the glow of everyone's congratulations – and Lana's mother's reiteration that I'm welcome to apply for membership of Domina Rei just as soon as I've turned eighteen – when Lars tugged on my sleeve (I guess the Domina Reis do let men into their events, if they're bodyguards) and said my grandmother had already passed out in the limo.

And that my father wanted to see me at once.

But whatever. Grandmere was just totally overcome with the emotion of finally being asked to join a club that has been snubbing her for the past fifty years. Because I totally saw Sophia Loren go up to her and issue an invitation to join. Grandmere practically fell over herself in her eagerness to say she'd think about it.

Which is princess for, 'I'll call you in the morning and say yes but I can't say it now or I'll look too eager.'

Dad yelled at me for like *half an hour* about how much I've let the family down and what a nightmare this is going to be with Parliament because it looks like our family has been hiding it all along and how now he's going to have to run for prime minister if he wants to continue any of the initiatives he's had planned and who even knows if he'll win if some of these other losers run and how the Genovian people are never going to be able to adjust to being a democracy and how now there'll be voter fraud and how I'll still have royal duties anyway only now I'll probably have to get a job some day because my allowance will be cut in half and he hopes I'm happy knowing I've basically just single-handedly destroyed a dynasty and am I aware that I'll be going down in history as the disgrace of the Renaldo family, until finally I was just like, 'Dad? You know what? You need to take it up with Dr Knutz. And you will, as a matter of fact, next Friday, when you and Grandmere accompany me to my appointment.'

THAT brought him up short. He looked all scared – like the time that flight attendant was claiming she was pregnant with his baby, until he realized he'd never met her before.

'Me?' he cried. 'Coming to one of your appointments? With my MOTHER?'

'Yes,' I said, not backing down. 'Because I really want to talk about how on your mental-health assessment you checked off *A little of the time* in answer to the statement *I feel as if true romantic love has passed me by* when just a couple of weeks ago you told me that you'll always regret having let Mom slip away. You totally lied to Dr Knutz, and you know if you lie in therapy – even to MY therapist – you're only hurting yourself, because how can you hope to make any progress if you're not honest with yourself first?'

Dad just blinked at me, I guess because I'd changed the subject so abruptly.

But then he went, looking all irritated, 'Mia, contrary to what you might like to believe in that over-romantic imagination of yours, I do not sit around pining for your mother every minute of every day. Yes, occasionally I regret that things didn't work out better with her. But life goes on. As you will find that life after Michael does. So, yes, I do feel that true love has passed me by, *A little of the time*. But the REST of the time I feel hopeful that new love might very well be waiting for me right around the next corner – as I hope it's waiting for

263

you as well. Now can we get back to the matter at hand? You had absolutely no right to do what you did tonight, and I'm very, very disappointed that you –'

But I didn't pay attention to the rest of what he said, because I was thinking about that phrase, *hopeful that new love might very well be waiting for me right around the next corner*.

How does someone make that transition? The transition from missing the person who they love so desperately that being without them feels like an empty ache inside their chest, to feeling hopeful that new love might very well be waiting for them right around the next corner?

I just don't know.

But I hope it happens to me some day . . .

Oh. We're on Thompson Street.

Great. As if my evening hasn't been eventful enough, now there is a homeless guy standing in our vestibule. Lars is getting out to remove him.

I hope he doesn't have to use the stun gun.

Saturday, September 25, 1 a.m., the Loft

It wasn't a homeless guy.

It was J.P.

He was waiting for me in the vestibule because it's so unseasonably cold out, he hadn't wanted to wait outside . . . and he hadn't wanted to buzz my mom and possibly wake her up.

But he'd wanted to see me because he'd watched the news about my speech on NY1.

And he'd wanted to make sure I was all right.

So he came all the way downtown to do so.

'I mean,' he kept saying, 'it's kind of a big deal, like they're saying on the news. One minute you're a regular girl, and the next, you're a princess. And a few years later, you're a princess, and the next minute . . . you're not.'

'I'm still a princess,' I reassured him.

'You are?' He looked uncertain.

I nodded. 'I'll always be a princess,' I said. 'It's just that now I can be a princess with a regular job and an apartment and stuff. If I want.'

It was as I was explaining all this to him on the front stoop – after Lars had nearly tasered him because he too had mistaken him for a vagrant – that the strangest thing happened:

It started to snow.

I *know*. Just very lightly, and freakishly early in the year for snow in Manhattan, especially given global warming. But it was definitely cold enough. Not cold enough to stick or anything. But there was no denying the tiny white flakes that started falling from the pinky night sky (pink because the clouds were hanging so low

265

that the city lights were reflecting off them) as I was talking.

And something strange happened when I looked up at the snowflakes, feeling them fall gently on my face, while I was listening to J.P. explain that he was glad I was still a princess after all.

All of a sudden – just like that – I didn't feel that depressed any more.

I can't really explain it any other way. Ms Martinez would no doubt be disappointed in my lack of descriptive verbs.

But that's exactly how it happened. Suddenly, I didn't feel so sad.

Not like I was cured or anything.

But that I'd climbed a few more feet out of that big black hole, and could see the sky – clearly – again. It was only just out of reach, as opposed to being dozens of feet overhead. I was *almost* there . . .

And the most amazing thing?

That I'd done it all by myself.

And then, while J.P. was going, 'And I hope you don't think I'm stalking you, because I'm not, I just thought maybe you'd need a friend, since I'm pretty sure your dad probably isn't too pleased with you right now –' I realized I felt . . . happy.

Really. *Happy*.

Not over the moon or anything. Not ecstatic. Not joyous.

But that was such a welcome change from feeling sad all the time that I – completely spontaneously and without thinking about it – flung both my arms around J.P.'s neck and gave him a great big kiss on the lips.

He seemed really surprised. But he rallied at the last minute and ended up putting his arms around me too and kissing me back.

And the weirdest thing of all was . . . I actually *felt* something when his lips touched mine.

I'm pretty sure.

It wasn't anything at all like what I felt when Michael and I kissed.

But it was something.

Maybe it was just the two or three flakes of snow on my face.

But maybe – just maybe – it was what my dad had talked about. You know:

Hope.

I don't know. But it felt good.

Finally Lars cleared his throat and I let go of J.P.

Then J.P. said, looking embarrassed, 'Well, maybe I am stalking you a *little*. Can I stalk you some more tomorrow?'

I laughed. Then I said:

'Yes. Goodnight, J.P.'

And then I went inside.

Where I saw that I had two messages in my inbox.

The first was from Tina:

Dear Mia

Oh my God! I just saw it on the news! Mia, you're just like Drew! In Ever After, *when she came in with the wings on her back! Except instead of just looking beautiful at a party, you actually*

DID something. Like CARRYING A PRINCE AROUND ON YOUR BACK. Only better. CONGRATULATIONS!!!!!

Love

Tina

Then I clicked on the second message. It was from Michael.

As always, my heartbeat speeded up when I saw his name. I guess that's something that's never going to change.

But at least the temperature of my palms stayed the same.

In the text of his message was a link to the story about my dropping a bomb of my own, with a note underneath that read:

Dear Mia

Did you just ditch your throne and bring democracy to a country that's never known it?

Way to go, Thermopolis!

Michael

I laughed when I saw it. I couldn't help it.

And you know . . . it felt good to laugh about something Michael had said (or written). It seemed like it had been a long time since that had happened.

And then it occurred to me that maybe Michael and I *can* be friends – just friends. For now, anyway.

So this time, instead of delete, I hit *Reply*.
And then I wrote him back.

Ten Out of Ten

Princess Amelia Mignonette Grimaldi Thermopolis Renaldo (Mia)

invites you to an exclusive event to celebrate her 18th birthday and the FABULOUS last ever instalment of The Princess Diaries

Dress code: Glamorous and gorgeous. Tiaras optional. And, Lana Weinberger, don't forget your underwear!

Etiquette: No curtsying. No paps. No kissing Prince William.

Mia's princess training is almost over. She can climb out of a limo as elegantly as any European heir presumptive. Even Grandmere approves of her practically perfect boyfriend, J.P. So this is the final instalment, the very end, the last EVER entry in The Princess Diaries. After all, Mia's about to turn eighteen – it's time to leave childish things behind. Like:

1. Lying.
2. Therapy with Dr Knutz – Mia's so ready to move on!
3. Being Albert Einstein High's last and only unicorn*.
4. Thinking about Michael Moscovitz. I mean, come ON. He's in Japan. And, besides, Mia is TOTALLY in love with J.P.
5. Michael who?

* You have *so* got to read the book!

air head

meg cabot

She's a brainiac trapped inside the body of an airhead . . .

Teenagers Emerson Watts and Nikki Howard have nothing in common. Em's a tomboy-brainiac who couldn't care less about her looks. Nikki's a stunning supermodel; the world's most famous airhead. But a freak accident causes the girls' lives to collide in the most extraordinary way – and suddenly Em knows more about Nikki's life than the paparazzi ever have!

The first book in a spectacular, romantic NEW TRILOGY with a spine-tingling twist!

Avalon High

MEG CABOT

Avalon High, Ellie's new school, is pretty much what she'd expected. There's Lance, the hunky footballer; Jennifer, the cute cheerleader; Marco, the troublemaker. And then there's Will – the most gorgeous guy Ellie's ever met. She can hardly believe he likes HER.

When Will says he thinks he's met Ellie before, things start getting a little weird. A feeling that grows as Ellie discovers the strange bonds that entwine Will, Lance, Jen, Marco – and herself.

As darkness turns to danger, can Ellie stop the horrific chain of events that threatens to engulf them all . . .

HOW TO BE
Popular
Meg Cabot

Do you want to be popular?

Everyone wants to be popular – and Steph Landry wants
it more than most. Steph's been the least popular girl in
class ever since she spilt that red Super Big Gulp over
Lauren Moffat's white D&G miniskirt five years ago.

Does being popular matter?

It matters very much – to Steph. That's why this year she's
got a plan to get in with the It Crowd in no time flat. Her
secret weapon: an old book called – what else? – *How to
Be Popular*.

But don't forget the most important thing about popularity!

It's easy to become popular. It's a lot less easy staying that way.

JINX

Meg Cabot

Does Jinx have bad luck – or special powers?

Misfortune has followed Jean Honeychurch all her life –
which is why everyone calls her Jinx. And now her parents
have shipped her off to New York to stay with relatives –
including her sophisticated cousin, Tory – until the trouble
she's caused back home dies down.

Could she even be . . . a WITCH?

Tory is far too cool to bother with Jinx – until Jinx's
chronic bad luck wreaks havoc in Tory's perfect life. Only
then does Jinx discover that beneath Tory's big-city glam-
our lies a world of hatred and revenge. Now it seems that
the jinx that's driven Jean crazy may just be the only thing
that can save her life . . .

A selected list of titles available from Macmillan Children's Books

The prices shown below are correct at the time of going to press. However, Macmillan Publishers reserves the right to show new retail prices on covers, which may differ from those previously advertised.

Meg Cabot

The Princess Diaries	978-0-330-48205-9	£5.99
The Princess Diaries: Take Two	978-0-330-48206-6	£5.99
The Princess Diaries: Third Time Lucky	9780-330-48207-3	£5.99
The Princess Diaries: Mia goes Fourth	978-0-330-41544-6	£5.99
The Princess Diaries: Give Me Five	978-0-330-41551-4	£5.99
The Princess Diaries: Sixsational	978-0-330-42038-9	£5.99
The Princess Diaries: Seventh Heaven	978-0-330-44155-1	£5.99
The Princess Diaries: After Eight	978-0-330-44688-4	£5.99
All American Girl	978-0-330-41555-2	£5.99
All American Girl: Ready or Not	978-0-330-43834-6	£5.99
Avalon High	978-0-330-44687-7	£5.99
Jinx	978-1-4050-9239-5	£9.99
How to Be Popular	978-0-330-44406-4	£5.99
Tommy Sullivan Is a Freak	978-1-4050-8983-8	£9.99
Airhead	978-0-230-70019-2	£9.99

All Pan Macmillan titles can be ordered from our website, www.panmacmillan.com, or from your local bookshop and are also available by post from:

Bookpost, PO Box 29, Douglas, Isle of Man IM99 1BQ

Credit cards accepted. For details:
Telephone: 01624 677237
Fax: 01624 670923
Email: bookshop@enterprise.net
www.bookpost.co.uk

Free postage and packing in the United Kingdom